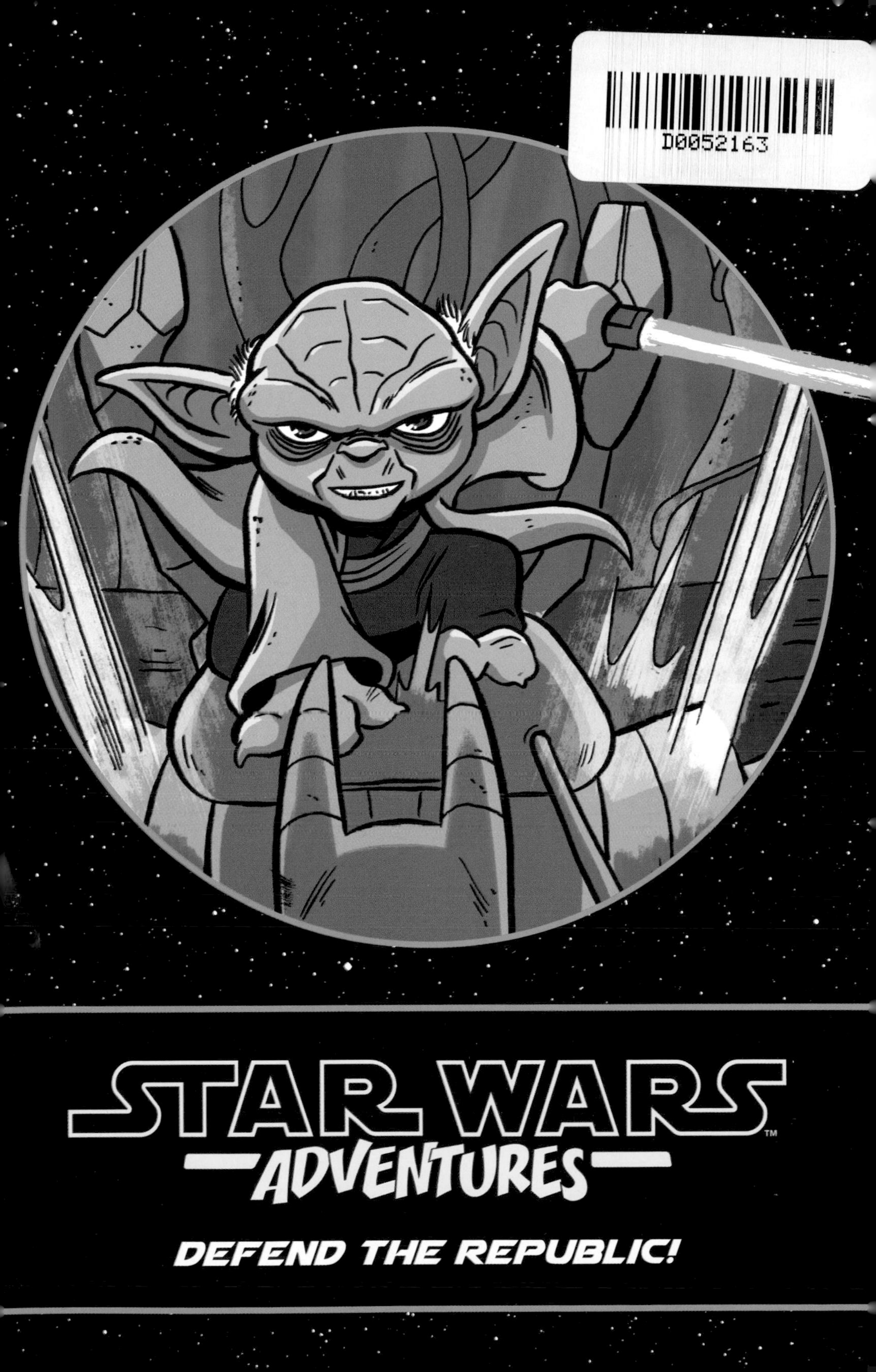

STAR WARS™ ADVENTURES

DEFEND THE REPUBLIC!

IDW

Facebook: **facebook.com/idwpublishing**
Twitter: **@idwpublishing**
YouTube: **youtube.com/idwpublishing**
Tumblr: **tumblr.idwpublishing.com**
Instagram: **instagram.com/idwpublishing**

COVER ARTIST
DEREK CHARM

LETTERER
TOM B. LONG

SERIES ASSISTANT EDITORS
ELIZABETH BREI
& ANNI PERHEENTUPA

SERIES EDITOR
DENTON J. TIPTON

COLLECTION EDITORS
JUSTIN EISINGER
& ALONZO SIMON

COLLECTION DESIGNER
CLYDE GRAPA

ISBN: 978-1-68405-619-4 23 22 21 20 1 2 3 4

STAR WARS ADVENTURES, VOLUME 8: DEFEND THE REPUBLIC. FEBRUARY 2020. FIRST PRINTING. IDW Publishing, a division of Idea and Design Works, LLC. Editorial offices: 2765 Truxtun Road, San Diego, CA 92106. Printed in Korea.

Originally published as STAR WARS ADVENTURES issues #18–20.

Disney · Lucasfilm

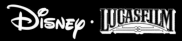

Lucasfilm Credits:
Robert Simpson, Senior Editor
Michael Siglain, Creative Director
Pablo Hidalgo, Matt Martin, and
Emily Shkoukani, Story Group

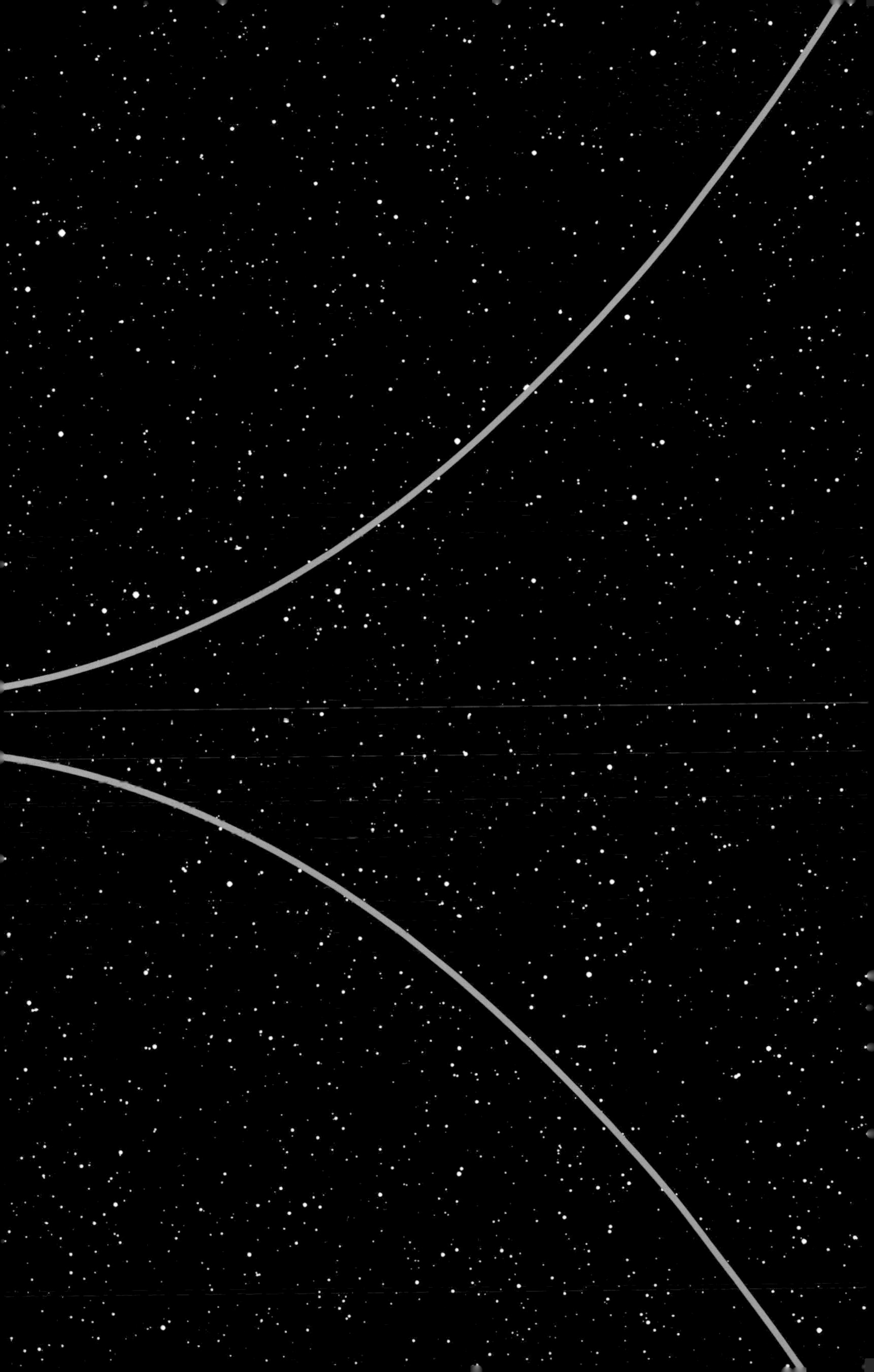

STAR WARS
ADVENTURES

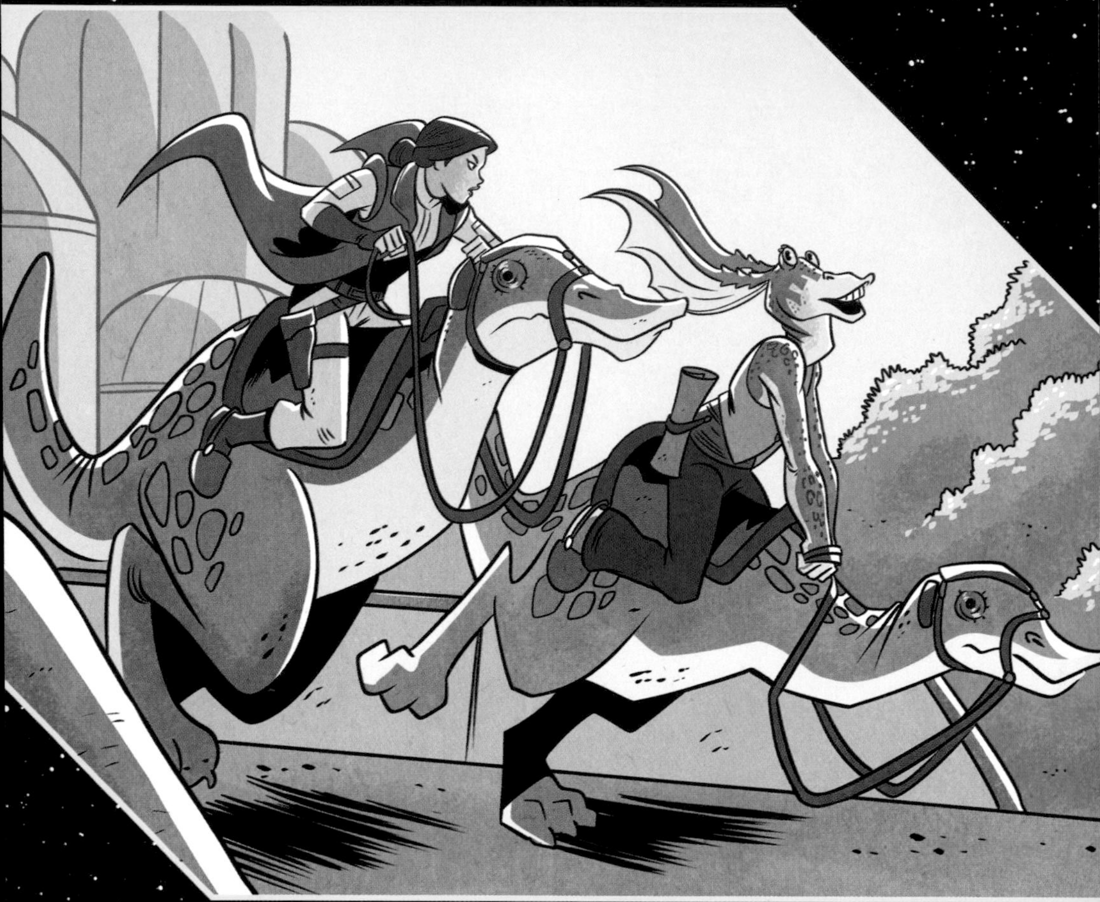

Raiders of the Lost Gundark

WRITER
DELILAH S. DAWSON
ARTIST & COLORIST
DEREK CHARM

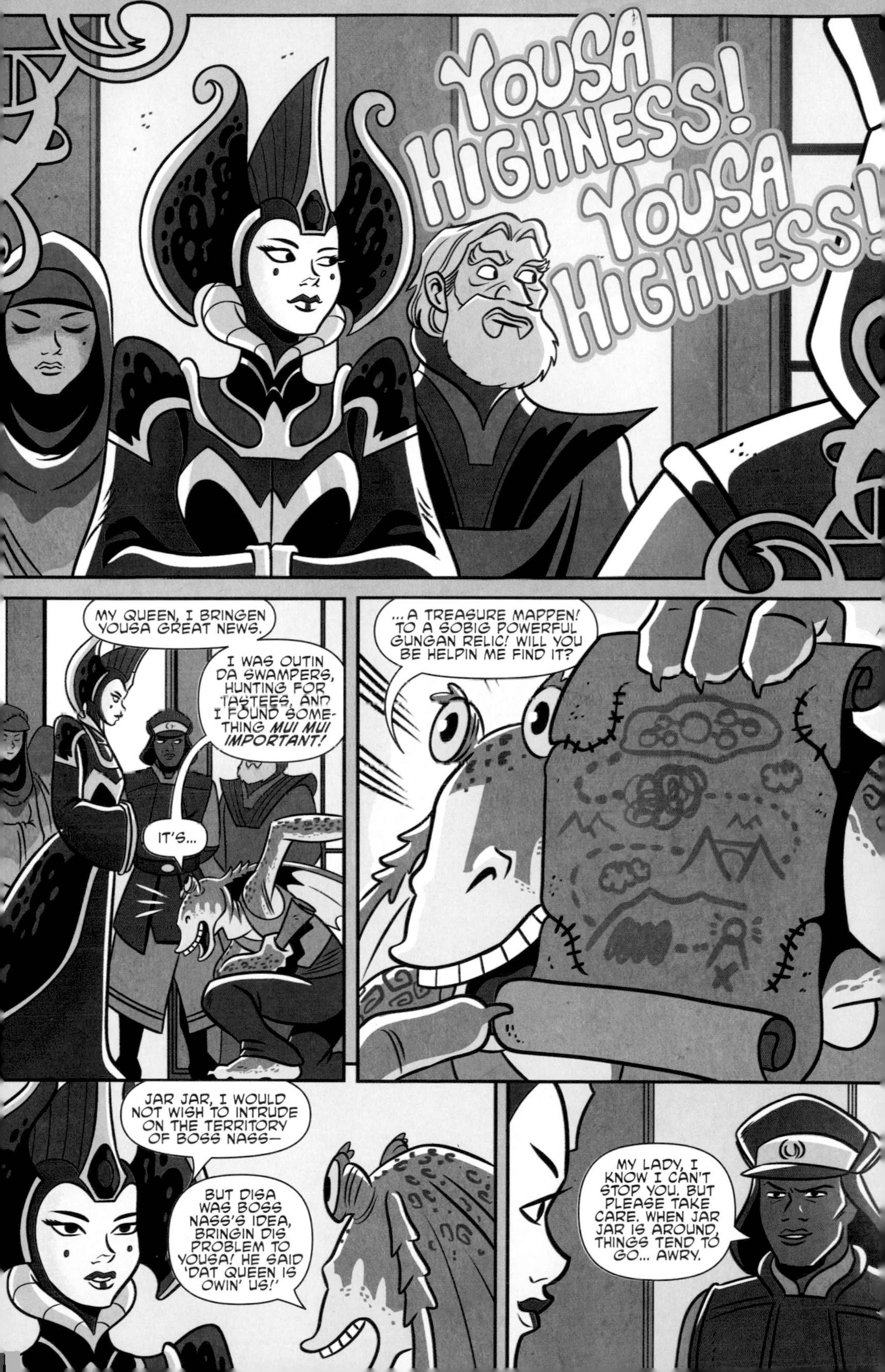
YOUSA HIGHNESS! YOUSA HIGHNESS!
MY QUEEN, I BRINGEN YOUSA GREAT NEWS.
I WAS OUTIN DA SWAMPERS, HUNTING FOR TASTEES, AND I FOUND SOMETHING *MUI MUI IMPORTANT!*
IT'S...
...A TREASURE MAPPEN! TO A SOBIG POWERFUL GUNGAN RELIC! WILL YOU BE HELPIN ME FIND IT?
JAR JAR, I WOULD NOT WISH TO INTRUDE ON THE TERRITORY OF BOSS NASS—
BUT DISA WAS BOSS NASS'S IDEA, BRINGIN DIS PROBLEM TO YOUSA! HE SAID 'DAT QUEEN IS OWIN' US!'
MY LADY, I KNOW I CAN'T STOP YOU. BUT PLEASE TAKE CARE. WHEN JAR JAR IS AROUND, THINGS TEND TO GO... AWRY.

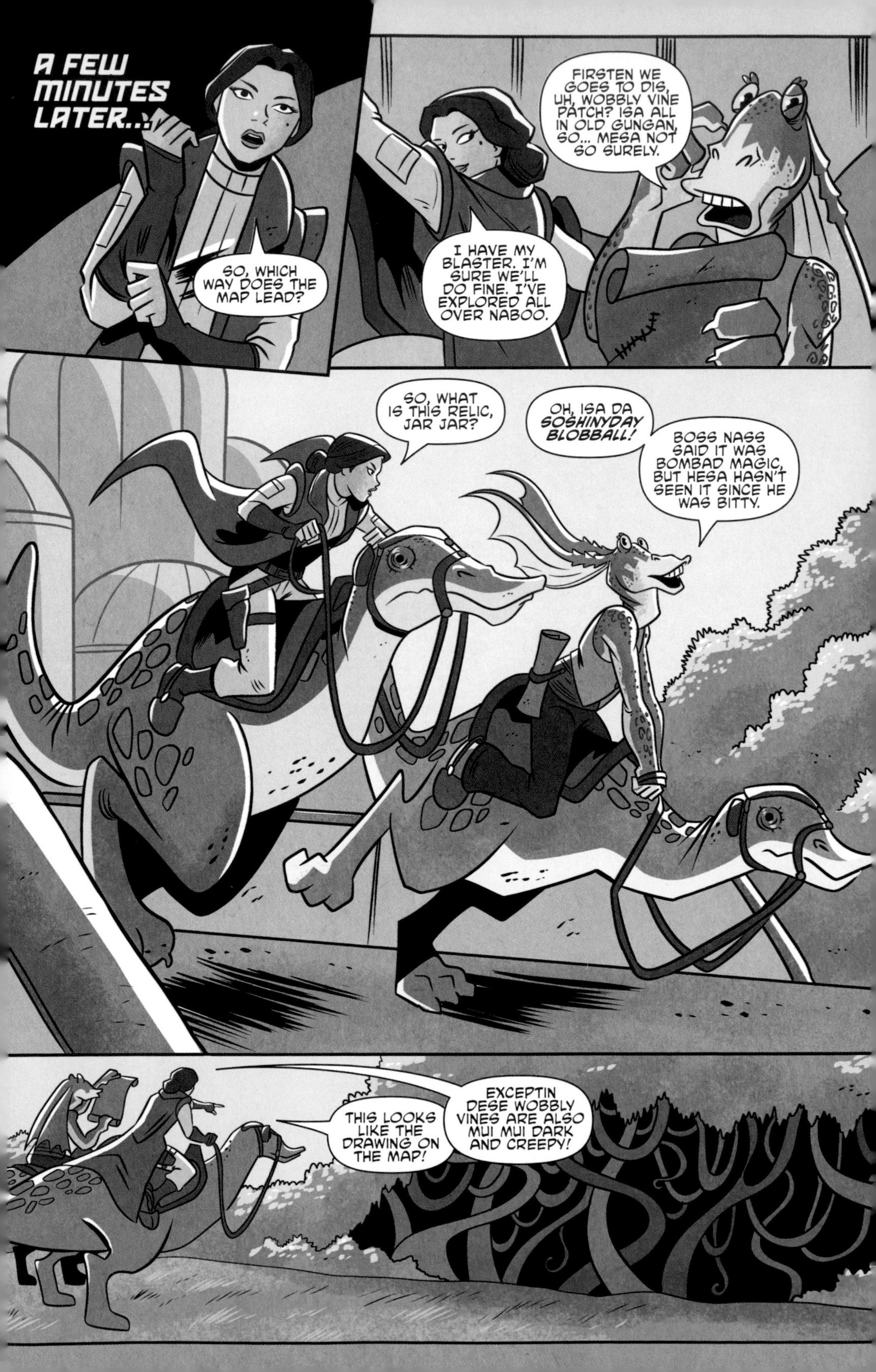
A FEW MINUTES LATER...
SO, WHICH WAY DOES THE MAP LEAD?
FIRSTEN WE GOES TO DIS, UH, WOBBLY VINE PATCH? ISA ALL IN OLD GUNGAN, SO... MESA NOT SO SURELY.
I HAVE MY BLASTER. I'M SURE WE'LL DO FINE. I'VE EXPLORED ALL OVER NABOO.
SO, WHAT IS THIS RELIC, JAR JAR?
OH, ISA DA SOSHINYDAY BLOBBALL!
BOSS NASS SAID IT WAS BOMBAD MAGIC, BUT HESA HASN'T SEEN IT SINCE HE WAS BITTY.
THIS LOOKS LIKE THE DRAWING ON THE MAP!
EXCEPTIN DESE WOBBLY VINES ARE ALSO MUI MUI DARK AND CREEPY!

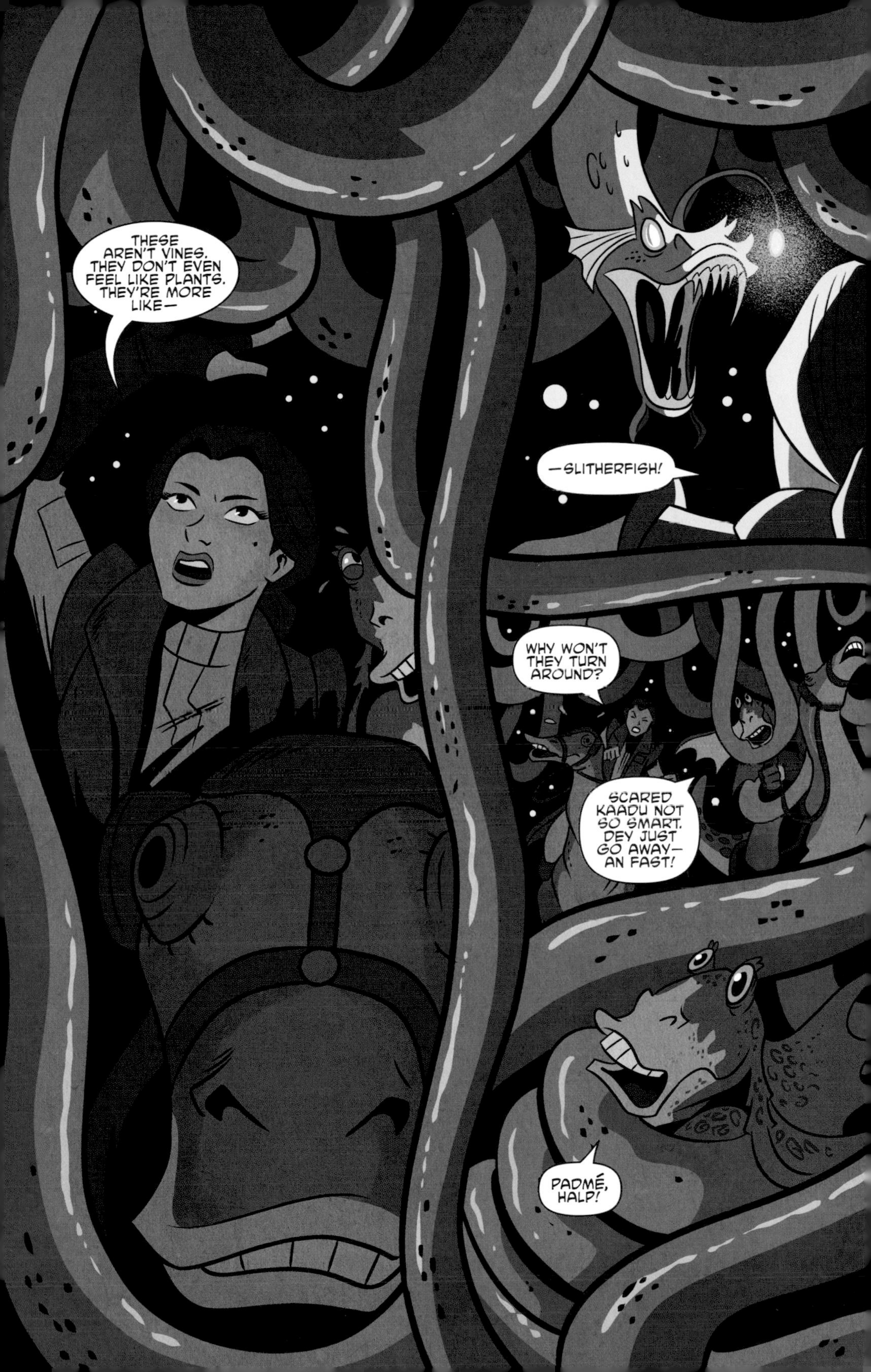
THESE AREN'T VINES. THEY DON'T EVEN FEEL LIKE PLANTS. THEY'RE MORE LIKE—
—SLITHERFISH!
WHY WON'T THEY TURN AROUND?
SCARED KAADU NOT SO SMART. DEY JUST GO AWAY—AN FAST!
PADMÉ, HALP!

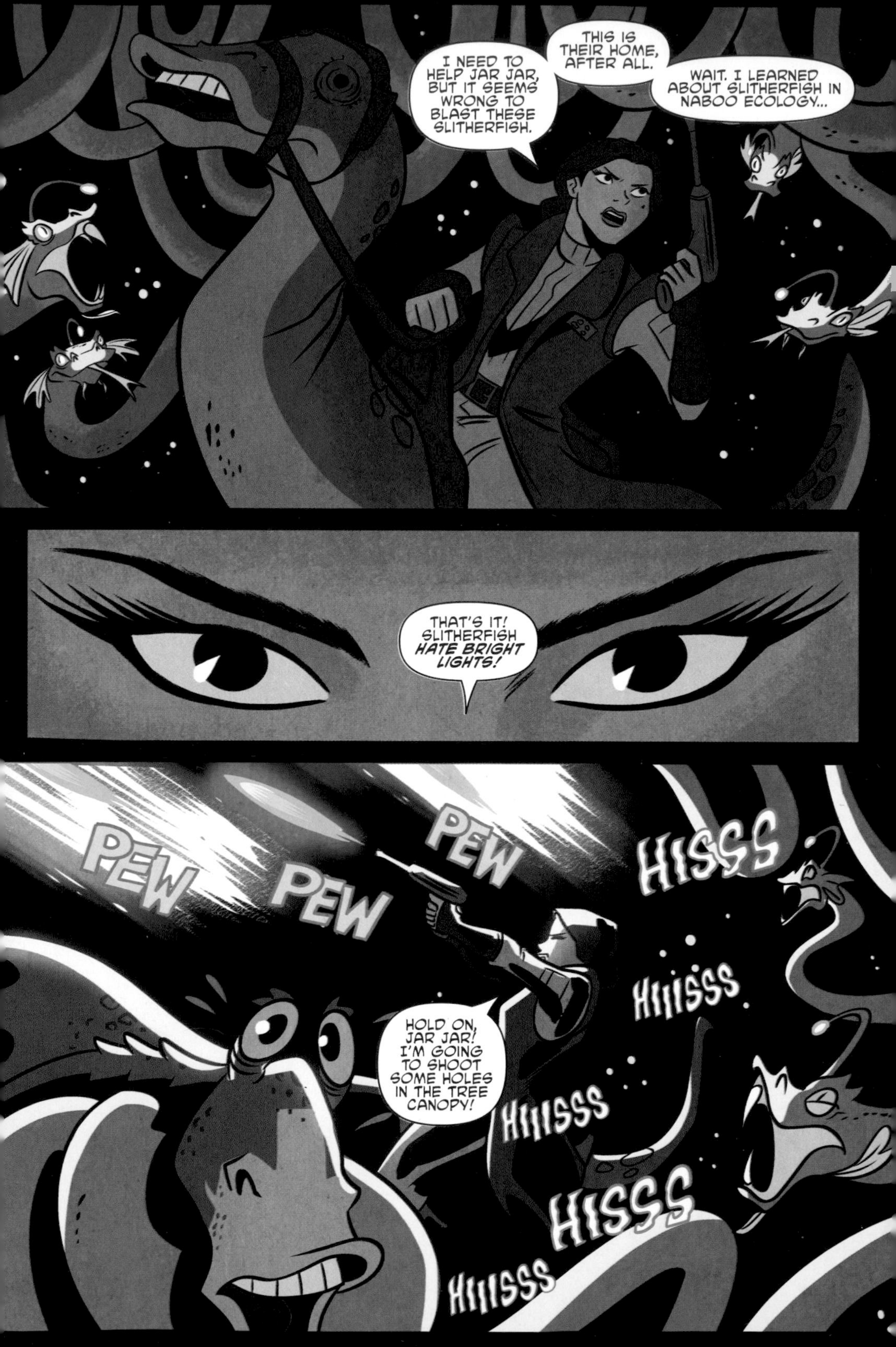
I NEED TO HELP JAR JAR, BUT IT SEEMS WRONG TO BLAST THESE SLITHERFISH.
THIS IS THEIR HOME, AFTER ALL.
WAIT. I LEARNED ABOUT SLITHERFISH IN NABOO ECOLOGY...
THAT'S IT! SLITHERFISH *HATE BRIGHT LIGHTS!*
PEW
PEW
PEW
HISSS
HIIISSS
HOLD ON, JAR JAR! I'M GOING TO SHOOT SOME HOLES IN THE TREE CANOPY!
HIIISSS
HISSS
HIIISSS

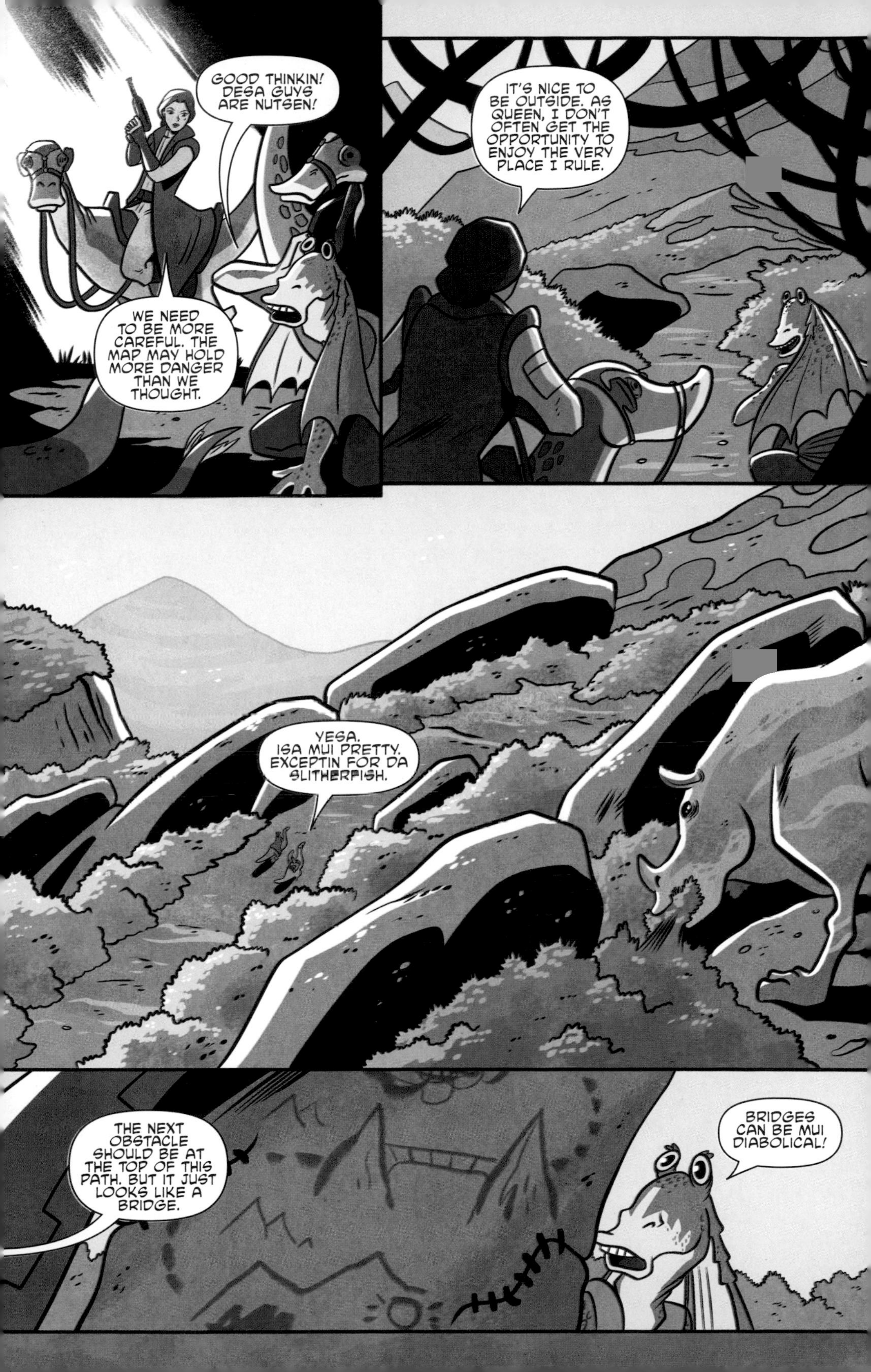
GOOD THINKIN! DESA GUYS ARE NUTSEN!
WE NEED TO BE MORE CAREFUL. THE MAP MAY HOLD MORE DANGER THAN WE THOUGHT.
IT'S NICE TO BE OUTSIDE. AS QUEEN, I DON'T OFTEN GET THE OPPORTUNITY TO ENJOY THE VERY PLACE I RULE.
YESA. ISA MUI PRETTY. EXCEPTIN FOR DA SLITHERFISH.
THE NEXT OBSTACLE SHOULD BE AT THE TOP OF THIS PATH. BUT IT JUST LOOKS LIKE A BRIDGE.
BRIDGES CAN BE MUI DIABOLICAL!

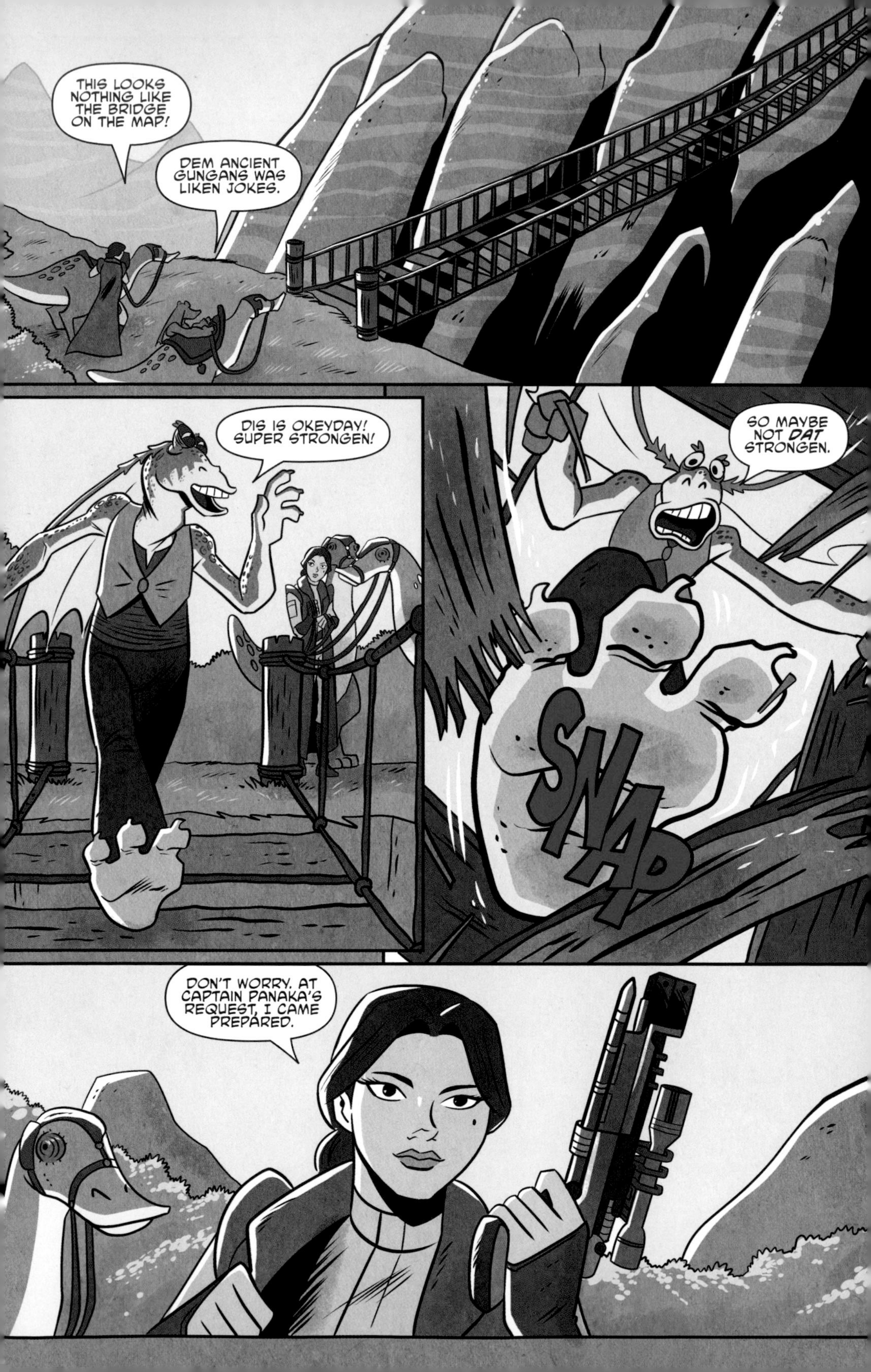
THIS LOOKS NOTHING LIKE THE BRIDGE ON THE MAP!
DEM ANCIENT GUNGANS WAS LIKEN JOKES.
DIS IS OKEYDAY! SUPER STRONGEN!
SO MAYBE NOT *DAT* STRONGEN.
SNAP
DON'T WORRY. AT CAPTAIN PANAKA'S REQUEST, I CAME PREPARED.

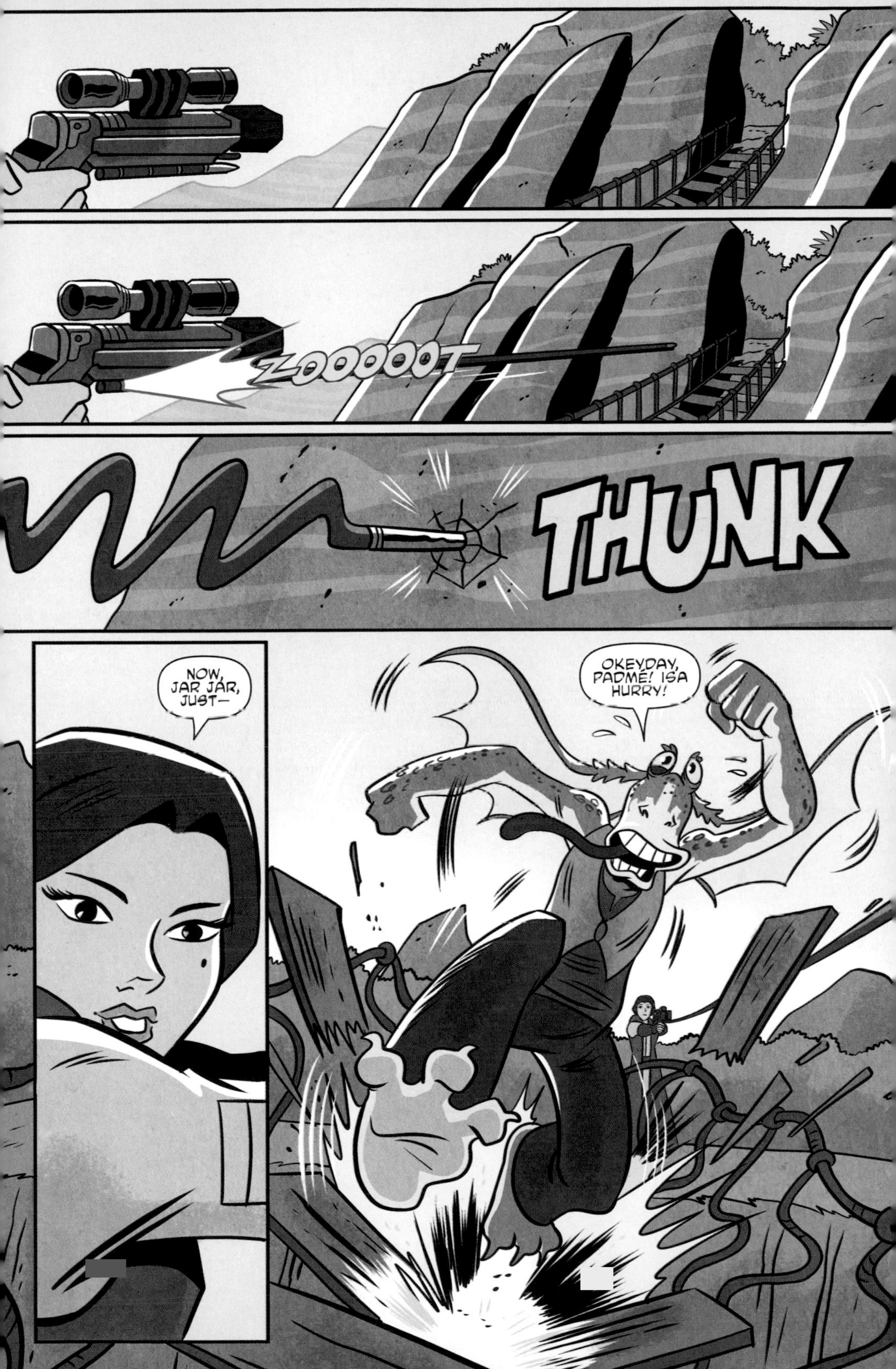
ZOOOOOT
THUNK
NOW, JAR JAR, JUST—
OKEYDAY, PADMÉ! ISA HURRY!

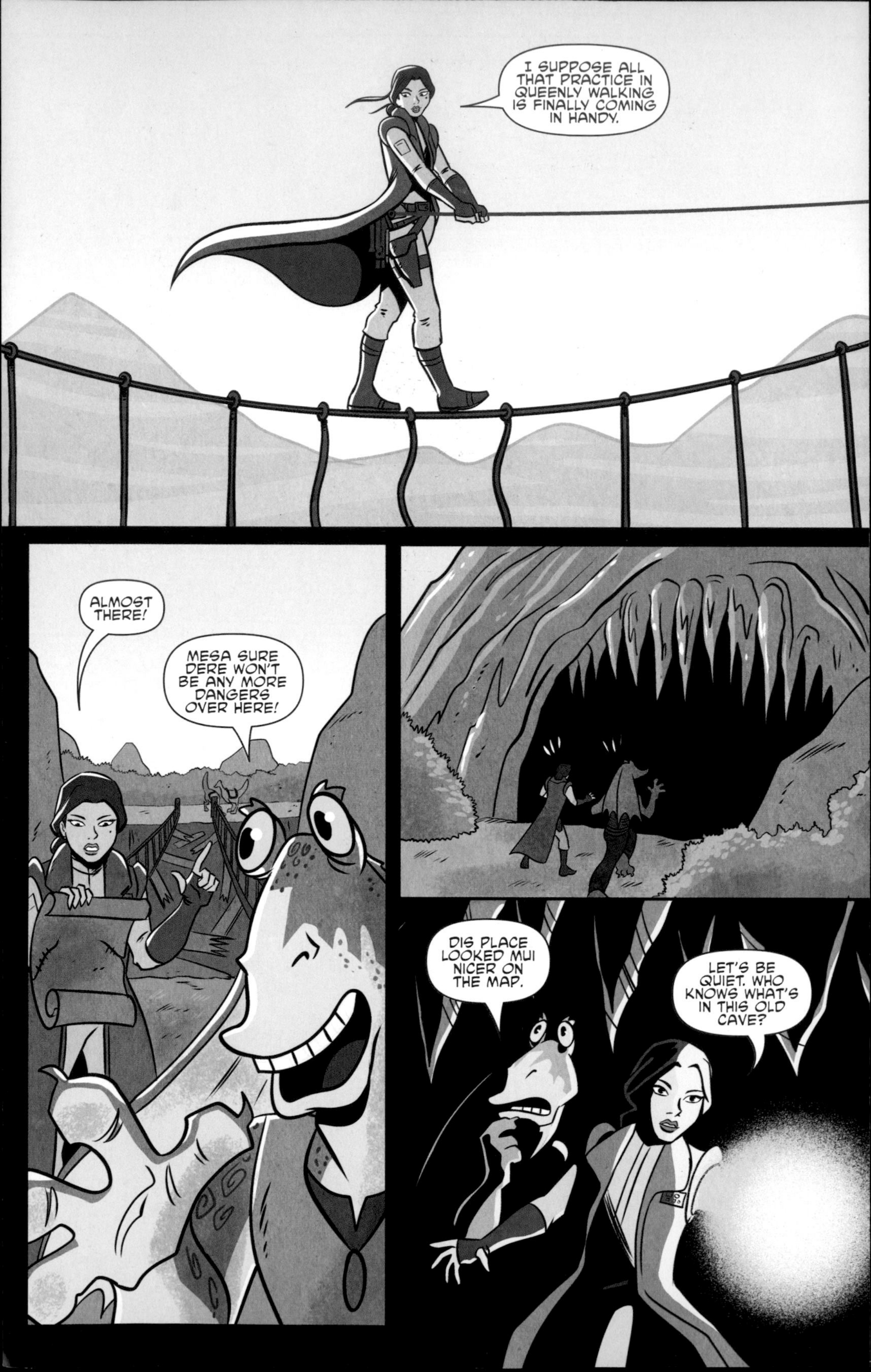
I SUPPOSE ALL THAT PRACTICE IN QUEENLY WALKING IS FINALLY COMING IN HANDY.
ALMOST THERE!
MESA SURE DERE WON'T BE ANY MORE DANGERS OVER HERE!
DIS PLACE LOOKED MUI NICER ON THE MAP.
LET'S BE QUIET. WHO KNOWS WHAT'S IN THIS OLD CAVE?

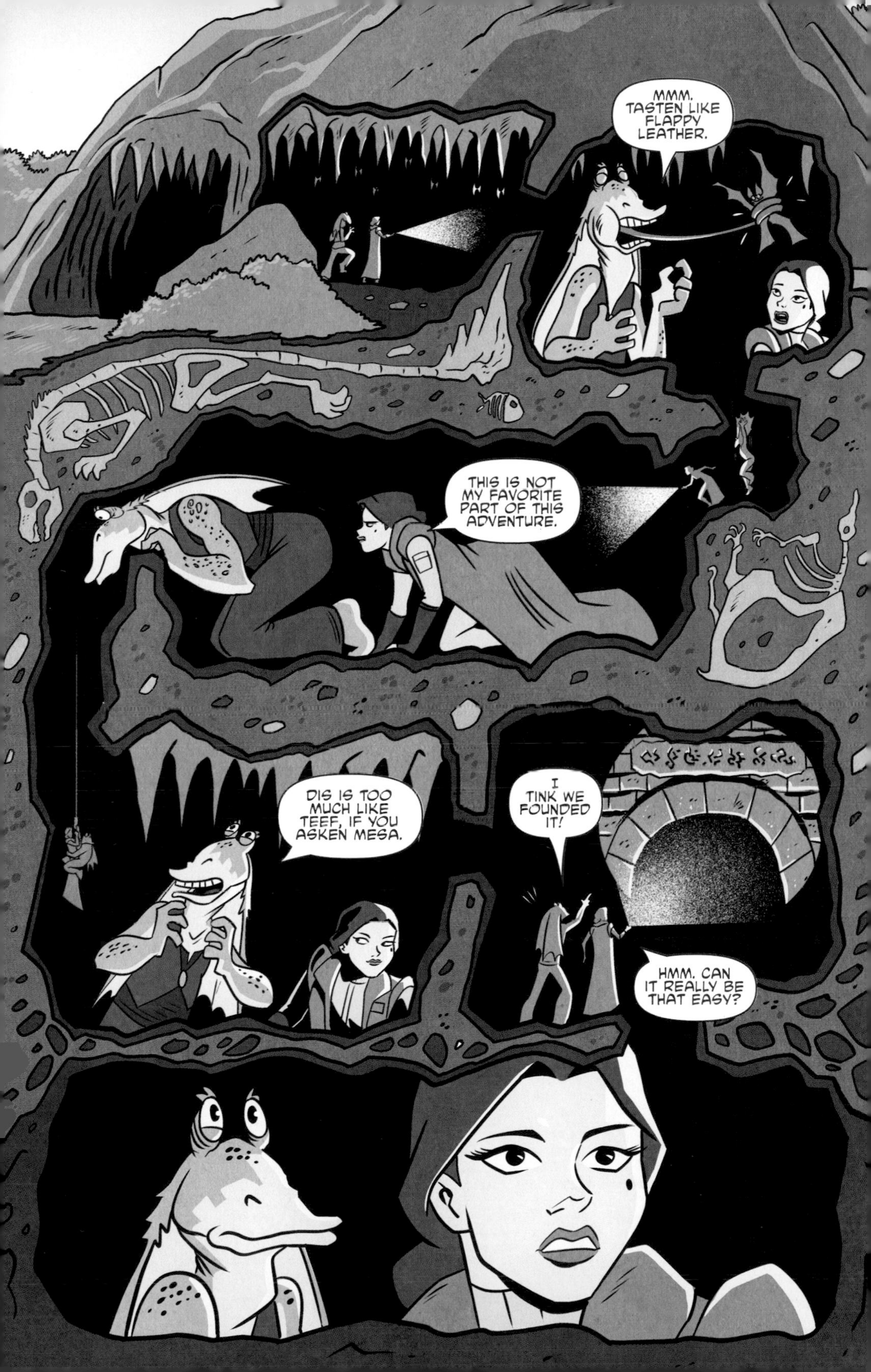
MMM. TASTEN LIKE FLAPPY LEATHER.
THIS IS NOT MY FAVORITE PART OF THIS ADVENTURE.
DIS IS TOO MUCH LIKE TEEF, IF YOU ASKEN MESA.
I TINK WE FOUNDED IT!
HMM. CAN IT REALLY BE THAT EASY?

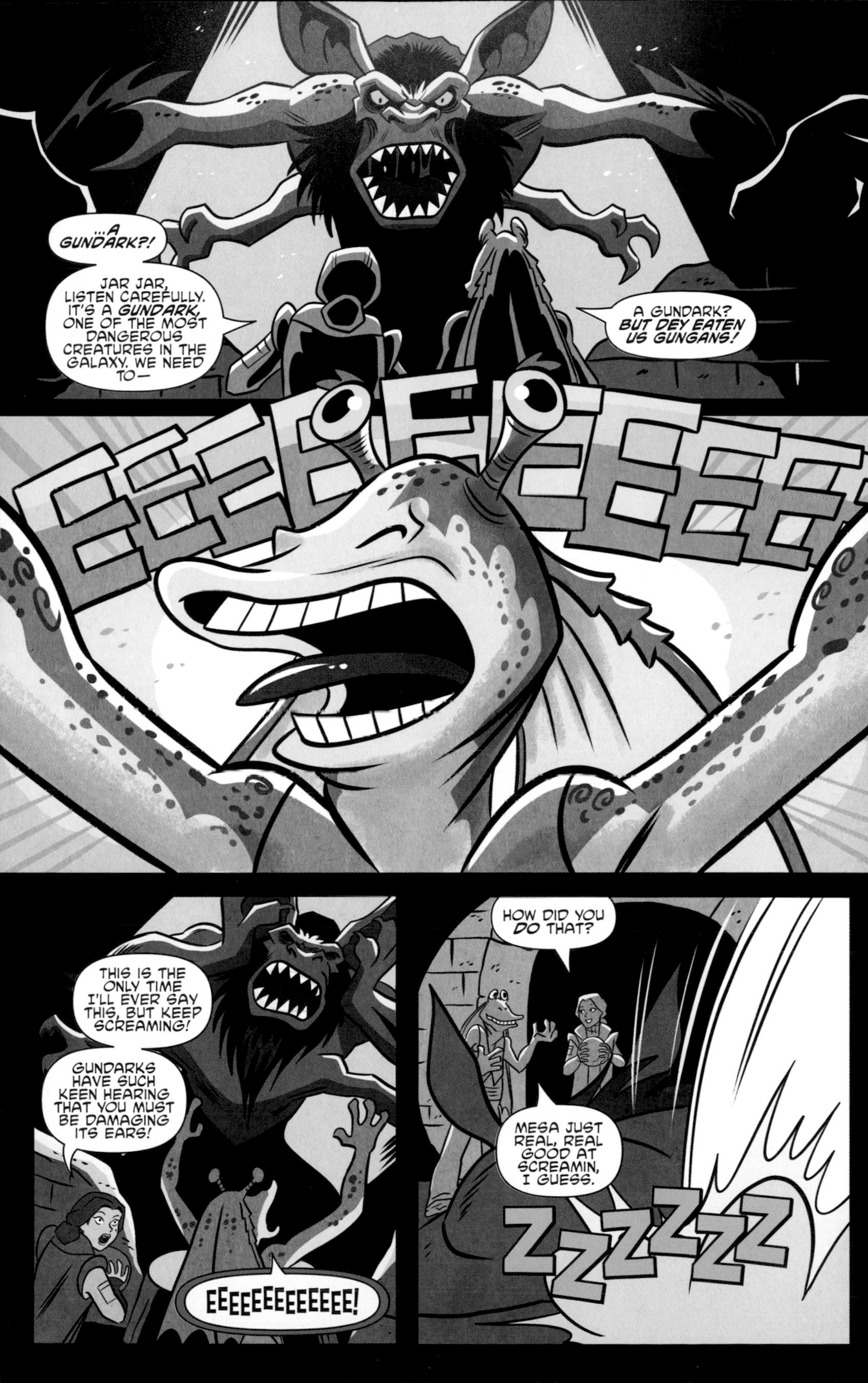
...A GUNDARK?!
JAR JAR, LISTEN CAREFULLY. IT'S A GUNDARK, ONE OF THE MOST DANGEROUS CREATURES IN THE GALAXY. WE NEED TO—
A GUNDARK? BUT DEY EATEN US GUNGANS!
EEEEEEEEEEEEEE
THIS IS THE ONLY TIME I'LL EVER SAY THIS, BUT KEEP SCREAMING!
GUNDARKS HAVE SUCH KEEN HEARING THAT YOU MUST BE DAMAGING ITS EARS!
EEEEEEEEEEEE!
HOW DID YOU DO THAT?
MESA JUST REAL, REAL GOOD AT SCREAMIN, I GUESS.
ZZZZZZ

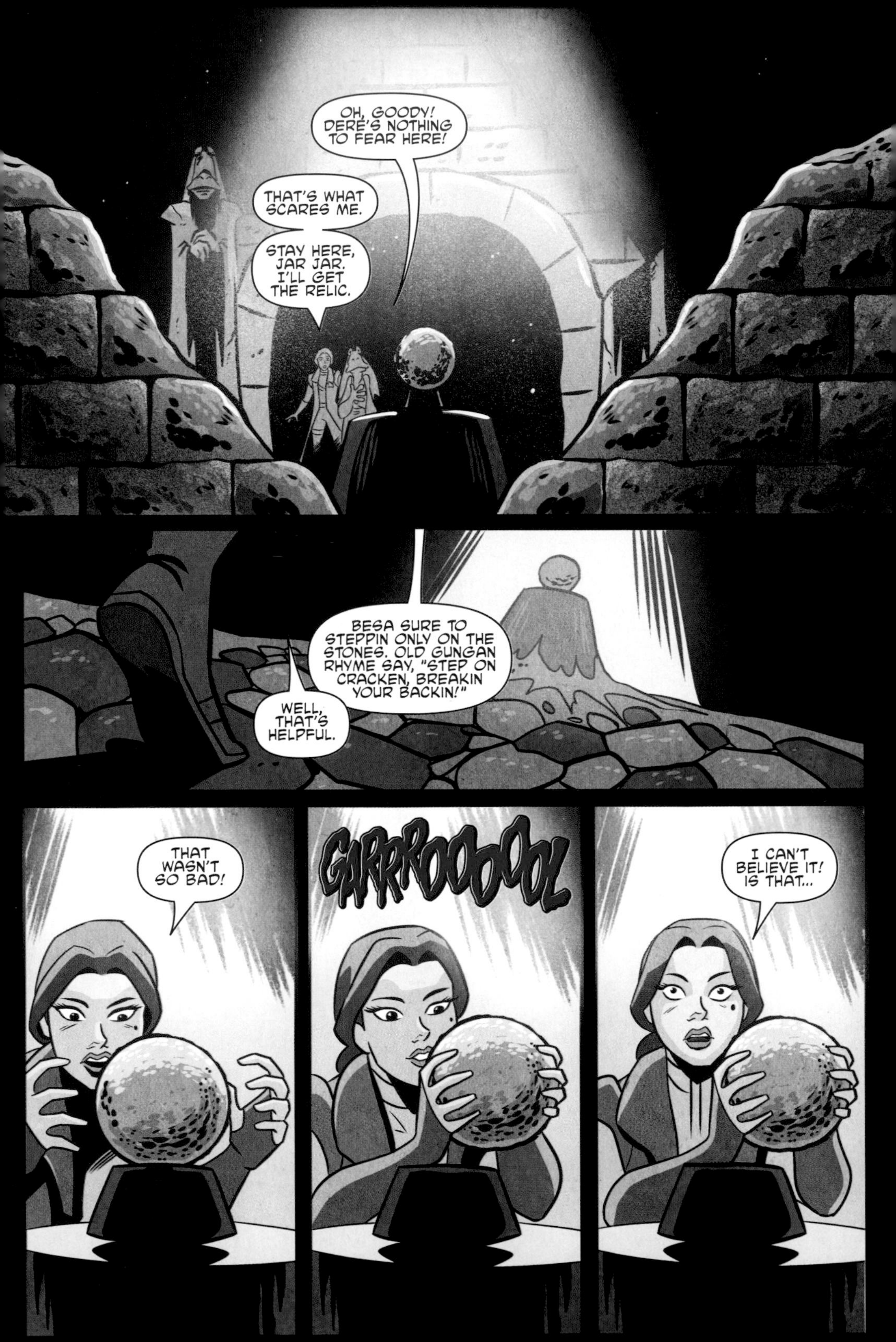
OH, GOODY! DERE'S NOTHING TO FEAR HERE!
THAT'S WHAT SCARES ME.
STAY HERE, JAR JAR. I'LL GET THE RELIC.
BESA SURE TO STEPPIN ONLY ON THE STONES. OLD GUNGAN RHYME SAY, "STEP ON CRACKEN, BREAKIN YOUR BACKIN!"
WELL, THAT'S HELPFUL.
THAT WASN'T SO BAD!
GARRROOOOOL
I CAN'T BELIEVE IT! IS THAT...

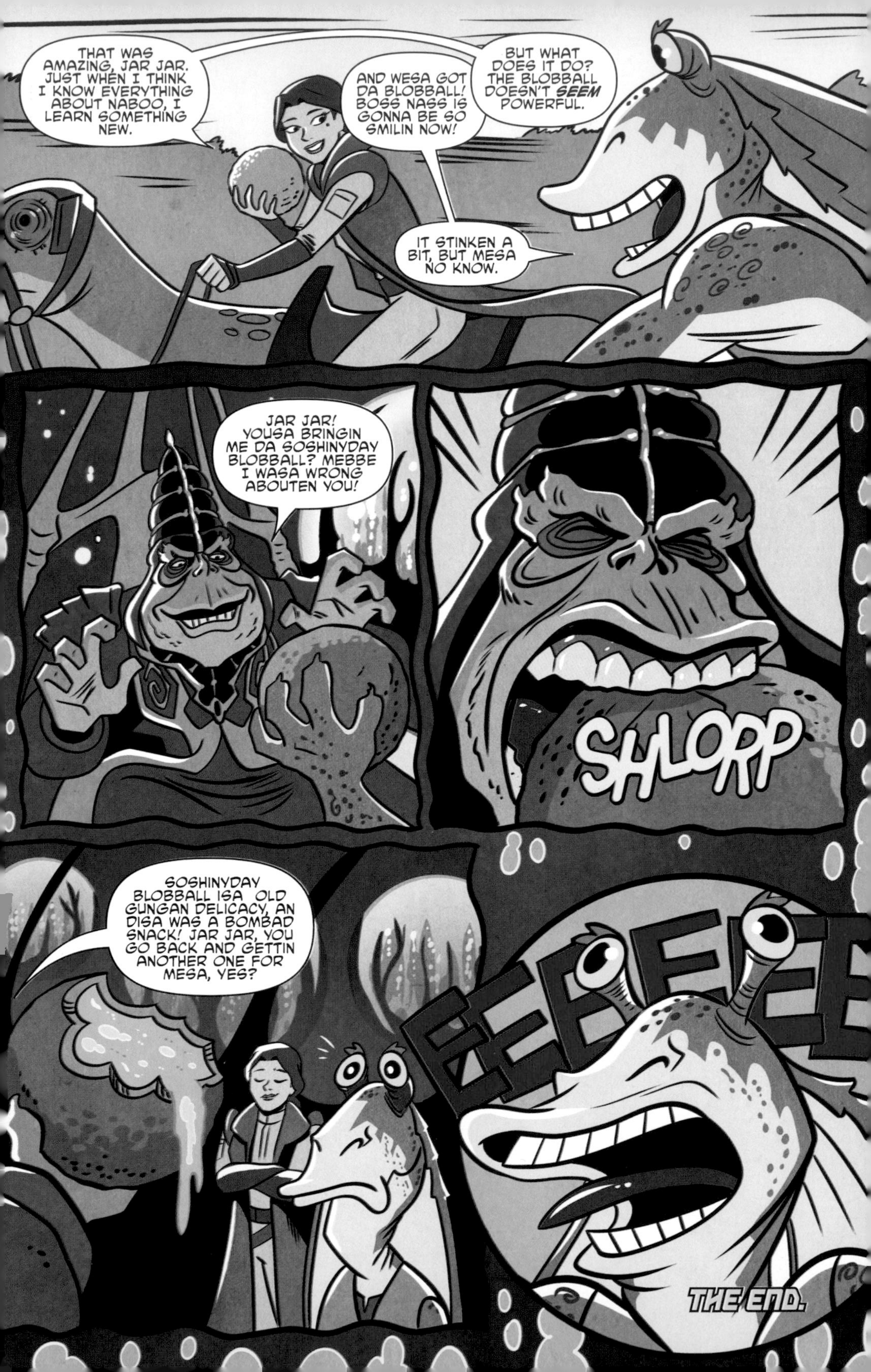
THAT WAS AMAZING, JAR JAR. JUST WHEN I THINK I KNOW EVERYTHING ABOUT NABOO, I LEARN SOMETHING NEW.
AND WESA GOT DA BLOBBALL! BOSS NASS IS GONNA BE SO SMILIN NOW!
BUT WHAT DOES IT DO? THE BLOBBALL DOESN'T SEEM POWERFUL.
IT STINKEN A BIT, BUT MESA NO KNOW.
JAR JAR! YOUSA BRINGIN ME DA SOSHINYDAY BLOBBALL? MEBBE I WASA WRONG ABOUTEN YOU!
SHLORP
SOSHINYDAY BLOBBALL ISA OLD GUNGAN DELICACY, AN DISA WAS A BOMBAD SNACK! JAR JAR, YOU GO BACK AND GETTIN ANOTHER ONE FOR MESA, YES?
EEEEE
THE END.

STAR WARS ADVENTURES

Roger Roger

WRITER
CAVAN SCOTT

ARTIST
MAURICET

COLORIST
CHARLIE KIRCHOFF

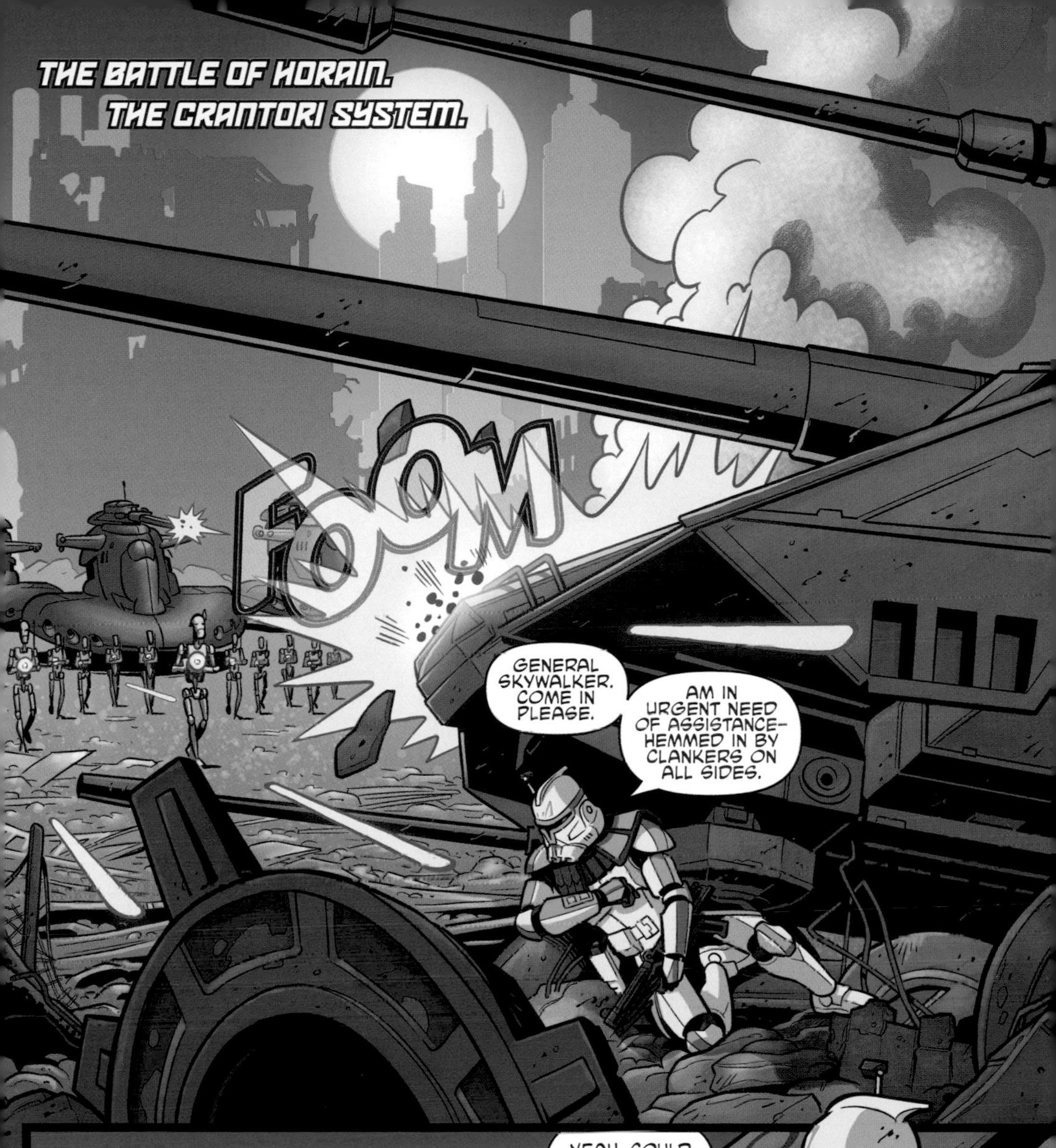
THE BATTLE OF HORAIN.
THE CRANTORI SYSTEM.
FOOM
GENERAL SKYWALKER. COME IN PLEASE.
AM IN URGENT NEED OF ASSISTANCE—HEMMED IN BY CLANKERS ON ALL SIDES.

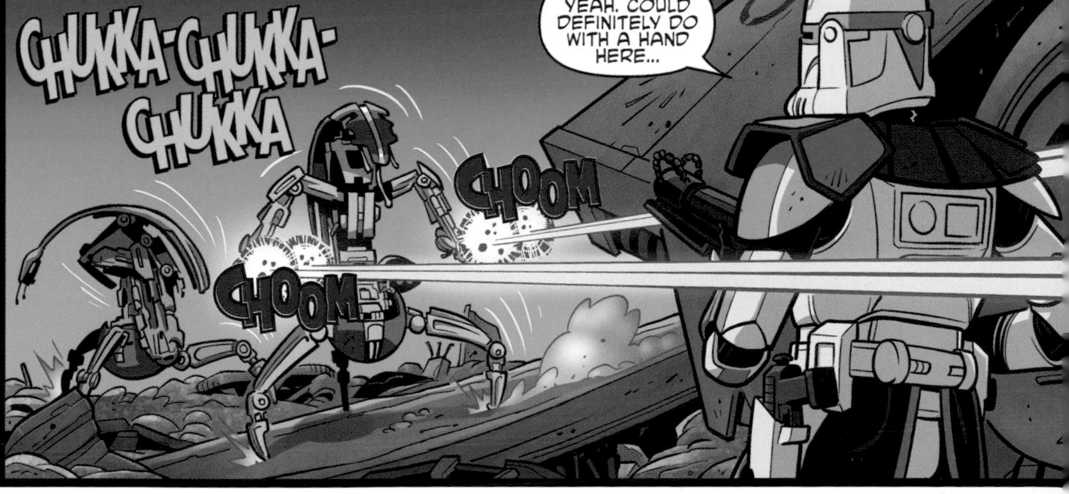
YEAH. COULD DEFINITELY DO WITH A HAND HERE...
CHUKKA-CHUKKA-CHUKKA
CHOOM
CHOOM

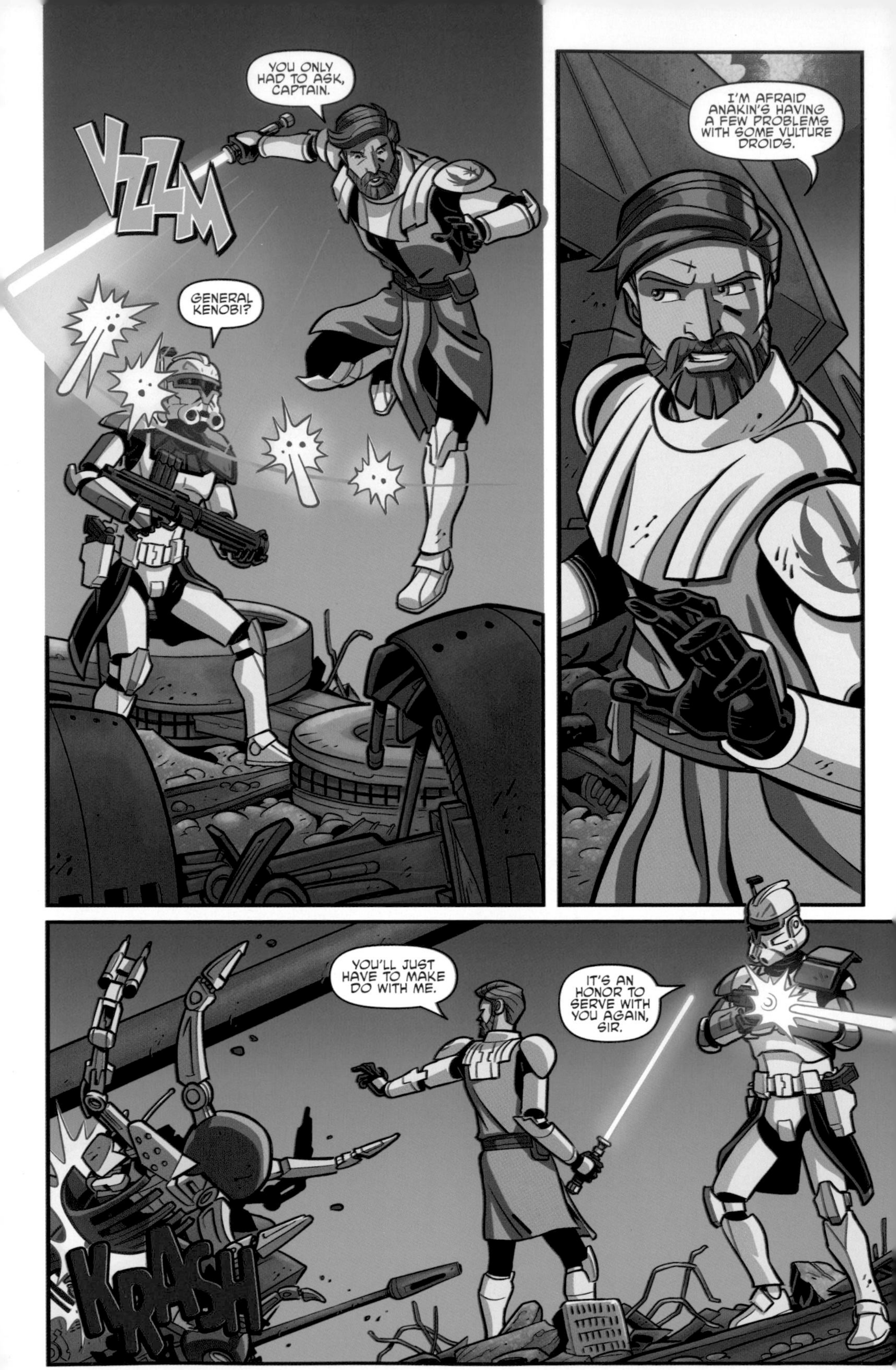
YOU ONLY HAD TO ASK, CAPTAIN.
VZZZM
GENERAL KENOBI?
I'M AFRAID ANAKIN'S HAVING A FEW PROBLEMS WITH SOME VULTURE DROIDS.
YOU'LL JUST HAVE TO MAKE DO WITH ME.
IT'S AN HONOR TO SERVE WITH YOU AGAIN, SIR.
KRASH

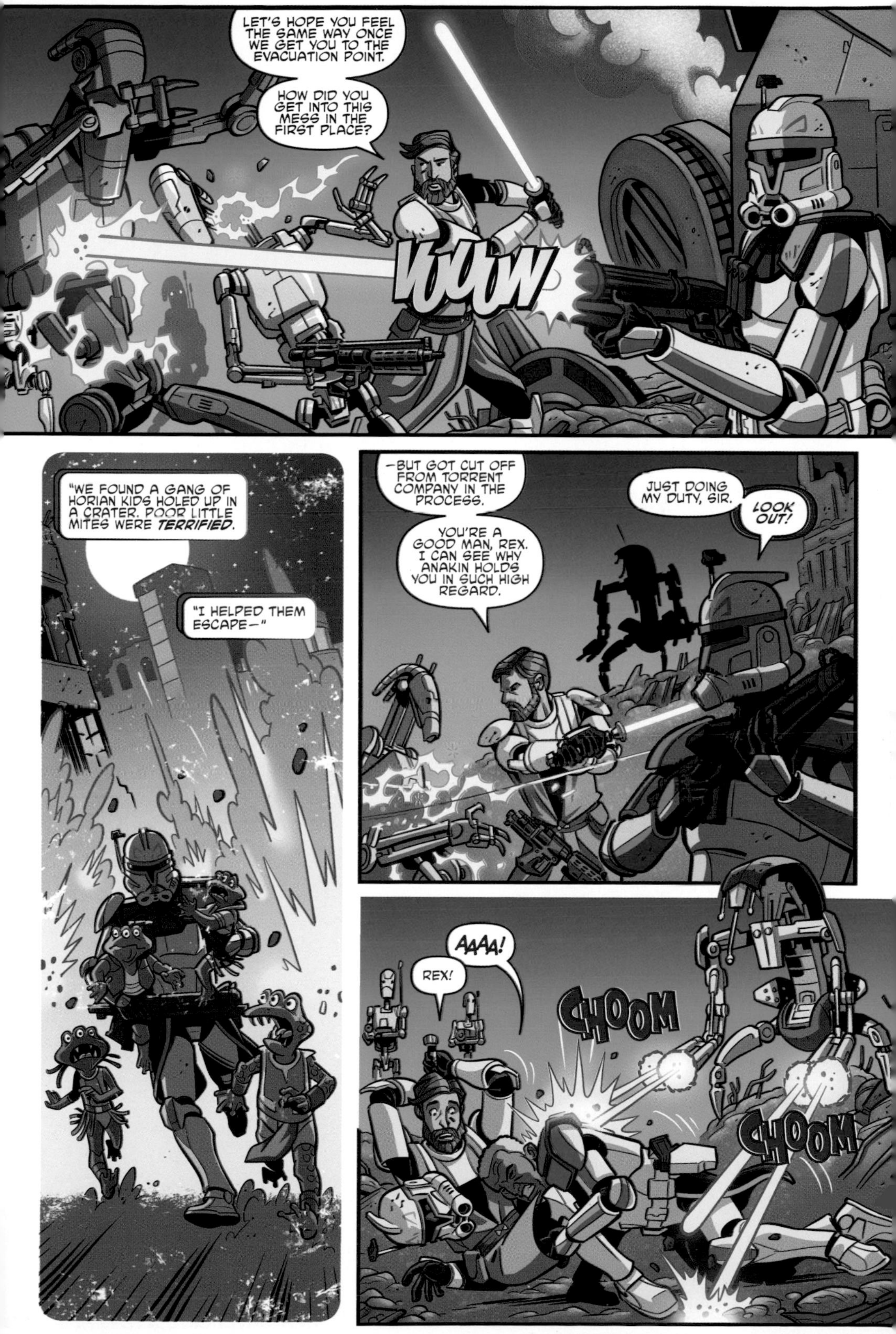
LET'S HOPE YOU FEEL THE SAME WAY ONCE WE GET YOU TO THE EVACUATION POINT.
HOW DID YOU GET INTO THIS MESS IN THE FIRST PLACE?
VVUUW
"WE FOUND A GANG OF HORIAN KIDS HOLED UP IN A CRATER. POOR LITTLE MITES WERE *TERRIFIED*.
"I HELPED THEM ESCAPE—"
—BUT GOT CUT OFF FROM TORRENT COMPANY IN THE PROCESS.
YOU'RE A GOOD MAN, REX. I CAN SEE WHY ANAKIN HOLDS YOU IN SUCH HIGH REGARD.
JUST DOING MY DUTY, SIR.
LOOK OUT!
AAAA!
REX!
CHOOM
CHOOM

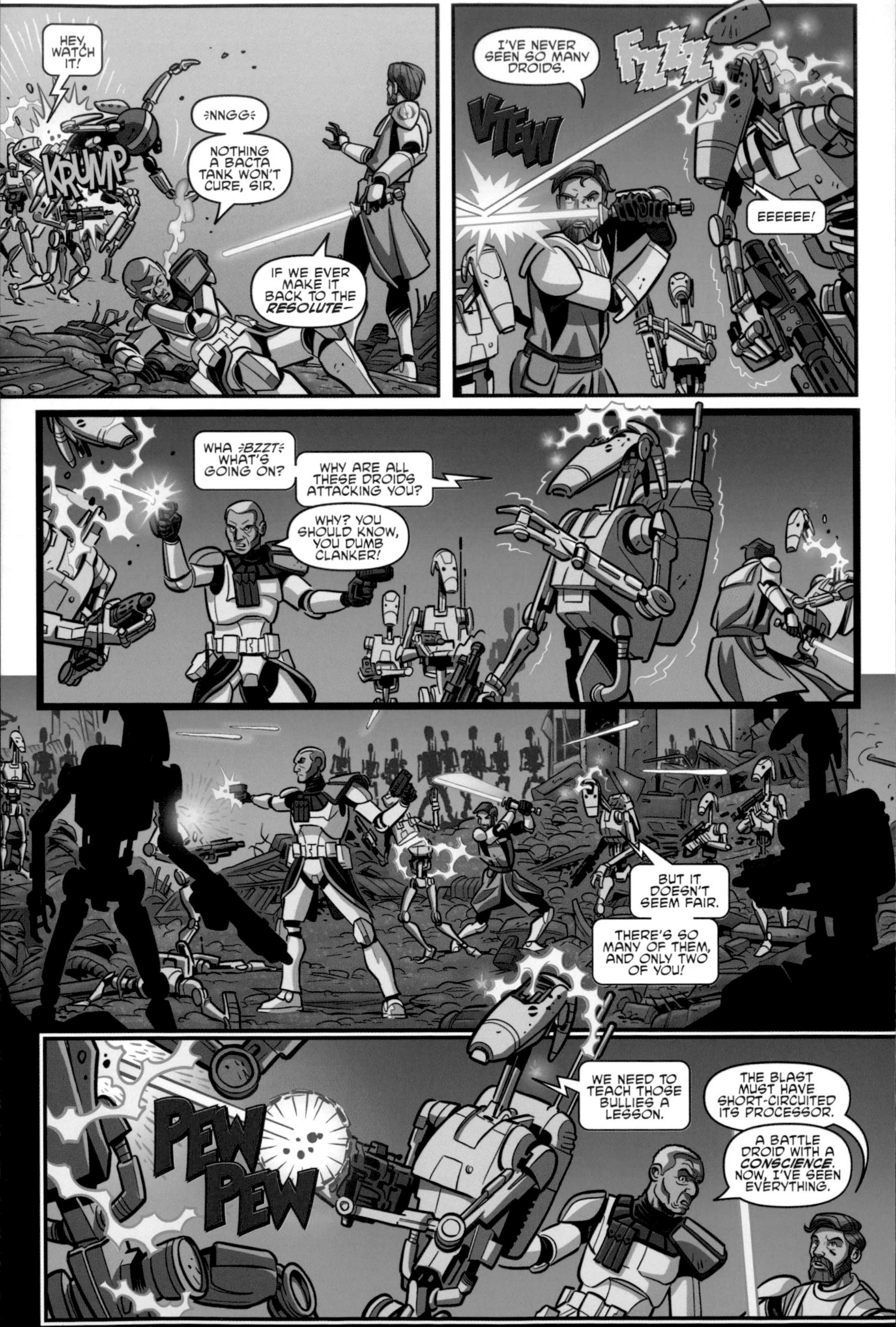
HEY, WATCH IT!
KRUMP
NNGG
NOTHING A BACTA TANK WON'T CURE, SIR.
IF WE EVER MAKE IT BACK TO THE RESOLUTE—
I'VE NEVER SEEN SO MANY DROIDS.
FZZZZ
VTEW
EEEEEE!
WHA BZZT WHAT'S GOING ON?
WHY ARE ALL THESE DROIDS ATTACKING YOU?
WHY? YOU SHOULD KNOW, YOU DUMB CLANKER!
BUT IT DOESN'T SEEM FAIR.
THERE'S SO MANY OF THEM, AND ONLY TWO OF YOU!
PEW PEW PEW
WE NEED TO TEACH THOSE BULLIES A LESSON.
THE BLAST MUST HAVE SHORT-CIRCUITED ITS PROCESSOR.
A BATTLE DROID WITH A CONSCIENCE. NOW, I'VE SEEN EVERYTHING.

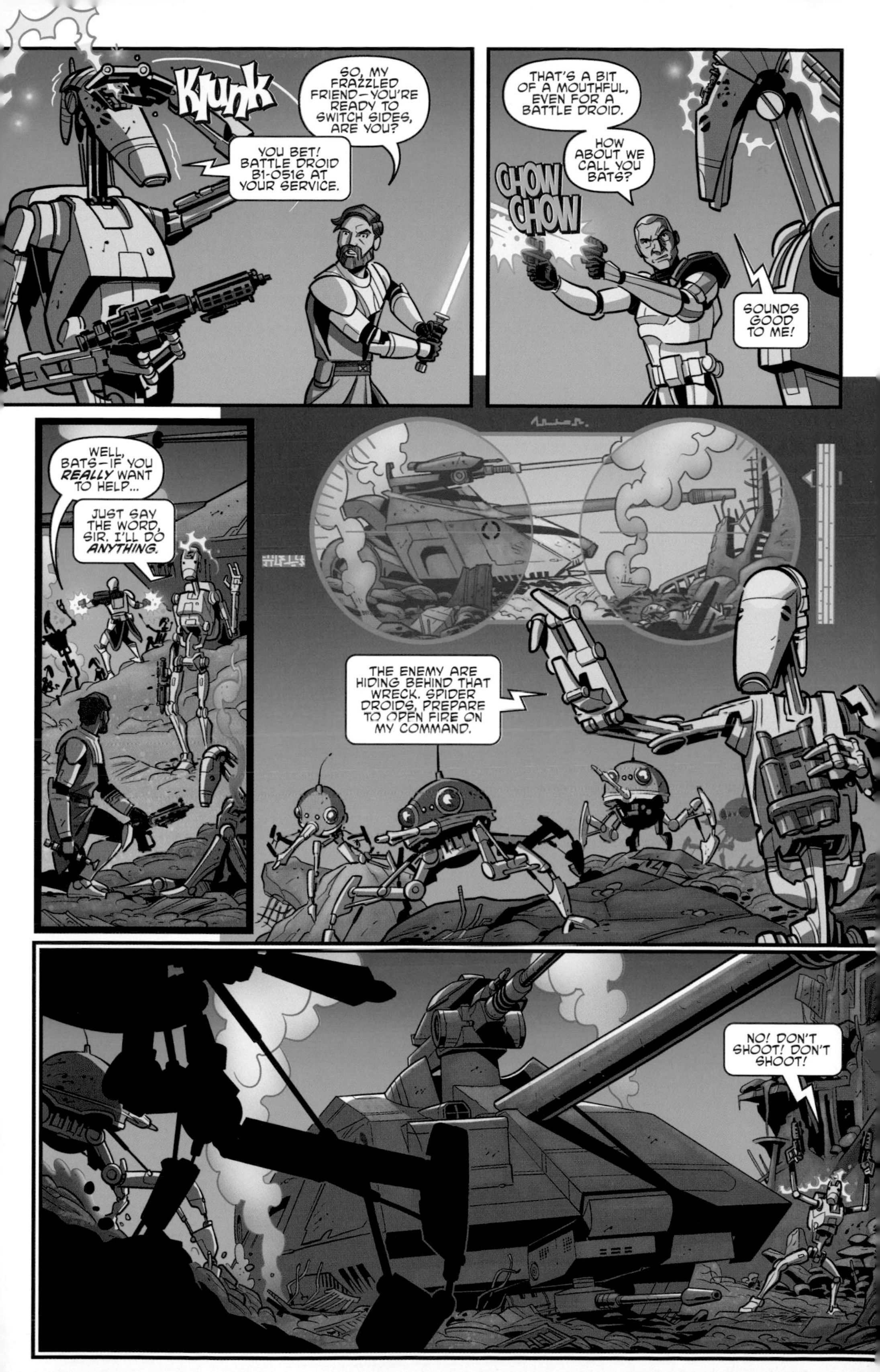
KLUNK
SO, MY FRAZZLED FRIEND—YOU'RE READY TO SWITCH SIDES, ARE YOU?
YOU BET! BATTLE DROID B1-0516 AT YOUR SERVICE.
THAT'S A BIT OF A MOUTHFUL, EVEN FOR A BATTLE DROID.
HOW ABOUT WE CALL YOU BATS?
CHOW CHOW
SOUNDS GOOD TO ME!
WELL, BATS—IF YOU *REALLY* WANT TO HELP...
JUST SAY THE WORD, SIR. I'LL DO *ANYTHING.*
THE ENEMY ARE HIDING BEHIND THAT WRECK. SPIDER DROIDS, PREPARE TO OPEN FIRE ON MY COMMAND.
NO! DON'T SHOOT! DON'T SHOOT!

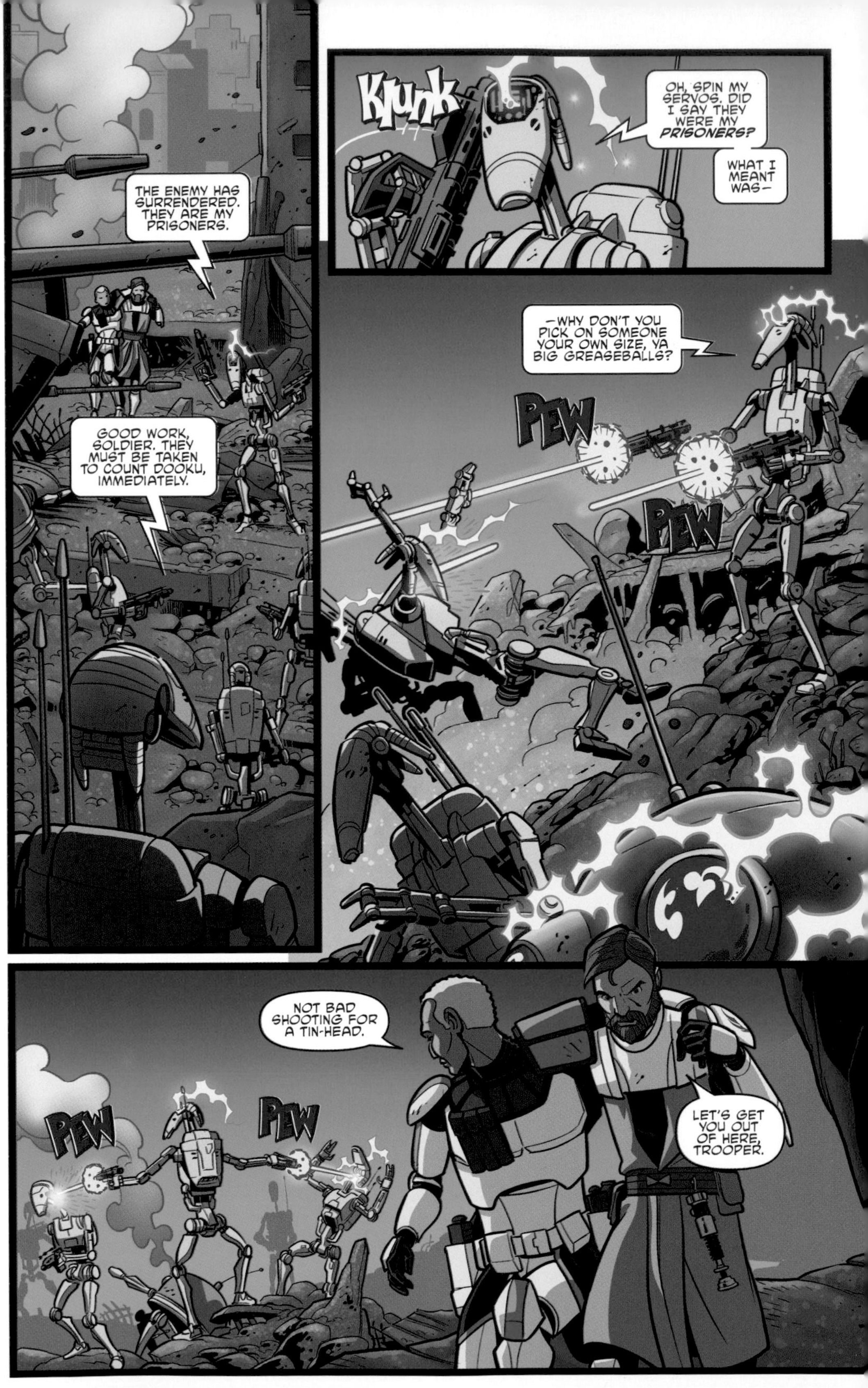
THE ENEMY HAS SURRENDERED. THEY ARE MY PRISONERS.
GOOD WORK, SOLDIER. THEY MUST BE TAKEN TO COUNT DOOKU, IMMEDIATELY.
KLUNK
OH, SPIN MY SERVOS. DID I SAY THEY WERE MY PRISONERS?
WHAT I MEANT WAS—
—WHY DON'T YOU PICK ON SOMEONE YOUR OWN SIZE, YA BIG GREASEBALLS?
PEW
PEW
NOT BAD SHOOTING FOR A TIN-HEAD.
LET'S GET YOU OUT OF HERE, TROOPER.
PEW
PEW

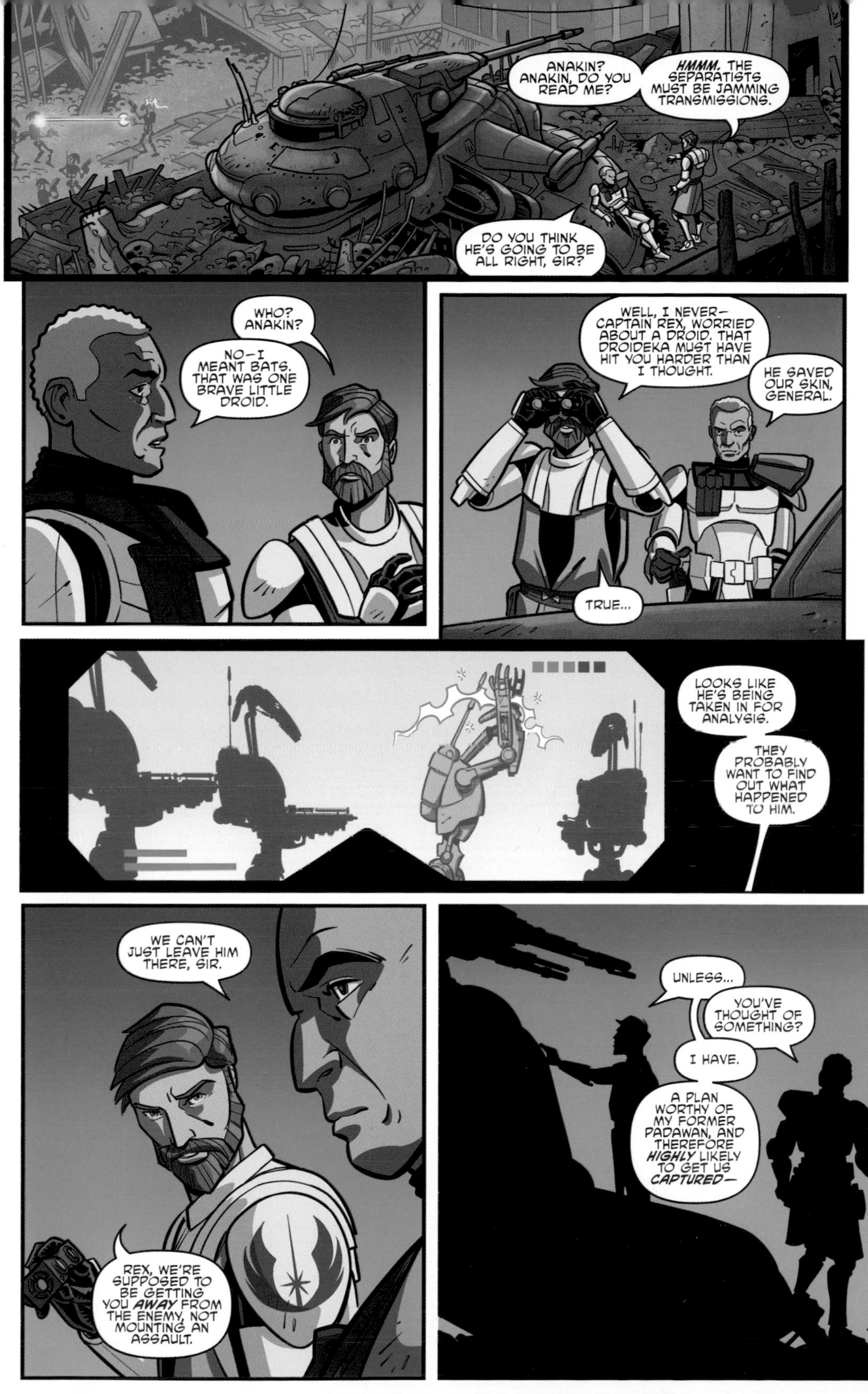
ANAKIN? ANAKIN, DO YOU READ ME?
HMMM. THE SEPARATISTS MUST BE JAMMING TRANSMISSIONS.
DO YOU THINK HE'S GOING TO BE ALL RIGHT, SIR?
WHO? ANAKIN?
NO—I MEANT BATS. THAT WAS ONE BRAVE LITTLE DROID.
WELL, I NEVER—CAPTAIN REX, WORRIED ABOUT A DROID. THAT DROIDEKA MUST HAVE HIT YOU HARDER THAN I THOUGHT.
HE SAVED OUR SKIN, GENERAL.
TRUE...
LOOKS LIKE HE'S BEING TAKEN IN FOR ANALYSIS.
THEY PROBABLY WANT TO FIND OUT WHAT HAPPENED TO HIM.
WE CAN'T JUST LEAVE HIM THERE, SIR.
REX, WE'RE SUPPOSED TO BE GETTING YOU AWAY FROM THE ENEMY, NOT MOUNTING AN ASSAULT.
UNLESS...
YOU'VE THOUGHT OF SOMETHING?
I HAVE.
A PLAN WORTHY OF MY FORMER PADAWAN, AND THEREFORE HIGHLY LIKELY TO GET US CAPTURED—

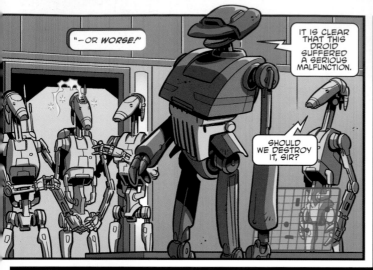

"—OR *WORSE!*"

IT IS CLEAR THAT THIS DROID SUFFERED A SERIOUS MALFUNCTION.

SHOULD WE DESTROY IT, SIR?

NO, IT CAN BE RETURNED TO SERVICE. THERE ARE PLENTY OF CLONE TROOPERS WHO STILL REQUIRE BLASTING.

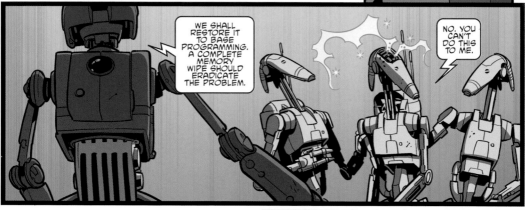

WE SHALL RESTORE IT TO BASE PROGRAMMING. A COMPLETE MEMORY WIPE SHOULD ERADICATE THE PROBLEM.

NO. YOU CAN'T DO THIS TO ME.

IT ISN'T *RIGHT!*

KLOK

B1-0516, YOU WILL SUBMIT TO REPROCESSING IMMEDIATELY.

THAT ISN'T EVEN MY NAME. I'M CALLED *BATS*, AND DON'T YOU FORGET IT!

VZZZT

OH, THIS IS HOPELESS.
CHANGE OF PLAN. BLOW ITS MALFUNCTIONING HEAD FROM ITS SHOULDERS.
YOU CAN TRY, YOU COWARDLY COG-HEADS.
I'LL TAKE YOU ALL, ONE-BY-ONE!
RUMBLE
NOW WHAT?
HAH! I KNEW YOU'D BE QUAKING IN YOUR BALANCE STABILIZERS.
FOOMFOOM
SIR, WE'RE UNDER ATTACK.
BUT THAT IS IMPOSSIBLE. REPUBLIC FORCES ARE NOWHERE NEAR THE GARRI—

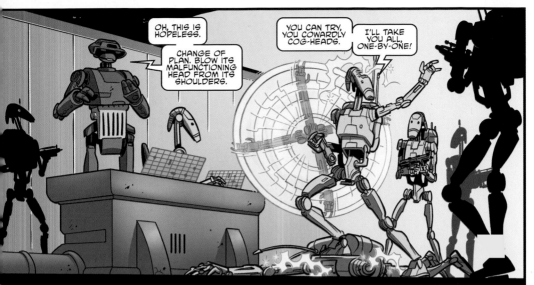

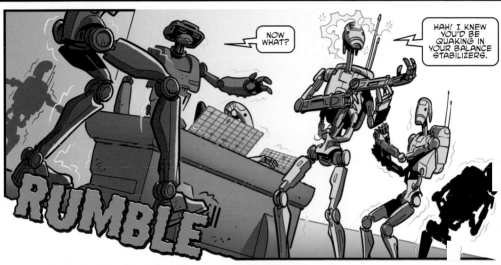

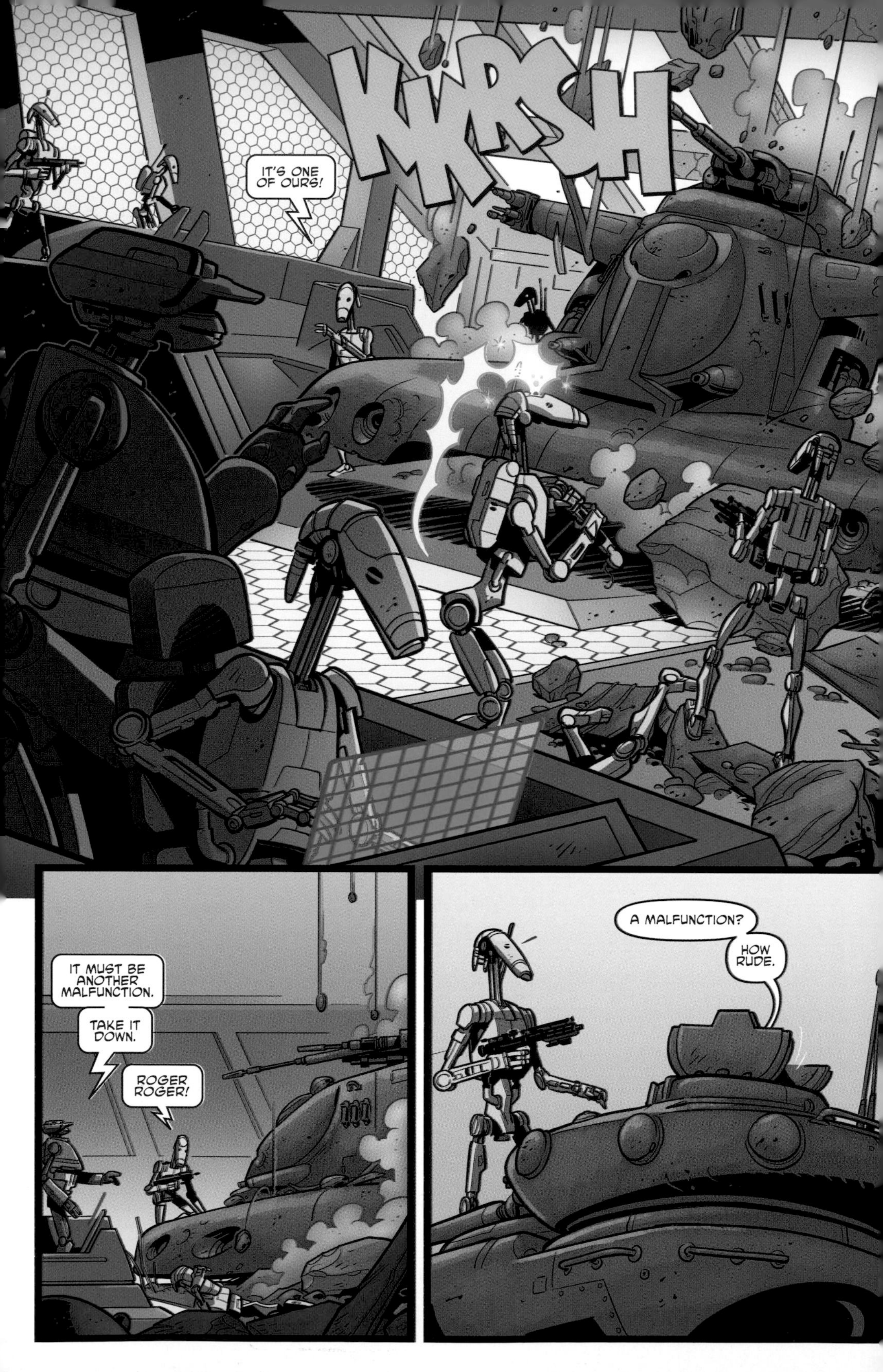
KWRSH
IT'S ONE OF OURS!
IT MUST BE ANOTHER MALFUNCTION.
TAKE IT DOWN.
ROGER ROGER!
A MALFUNCTION?
HOW RUDE.

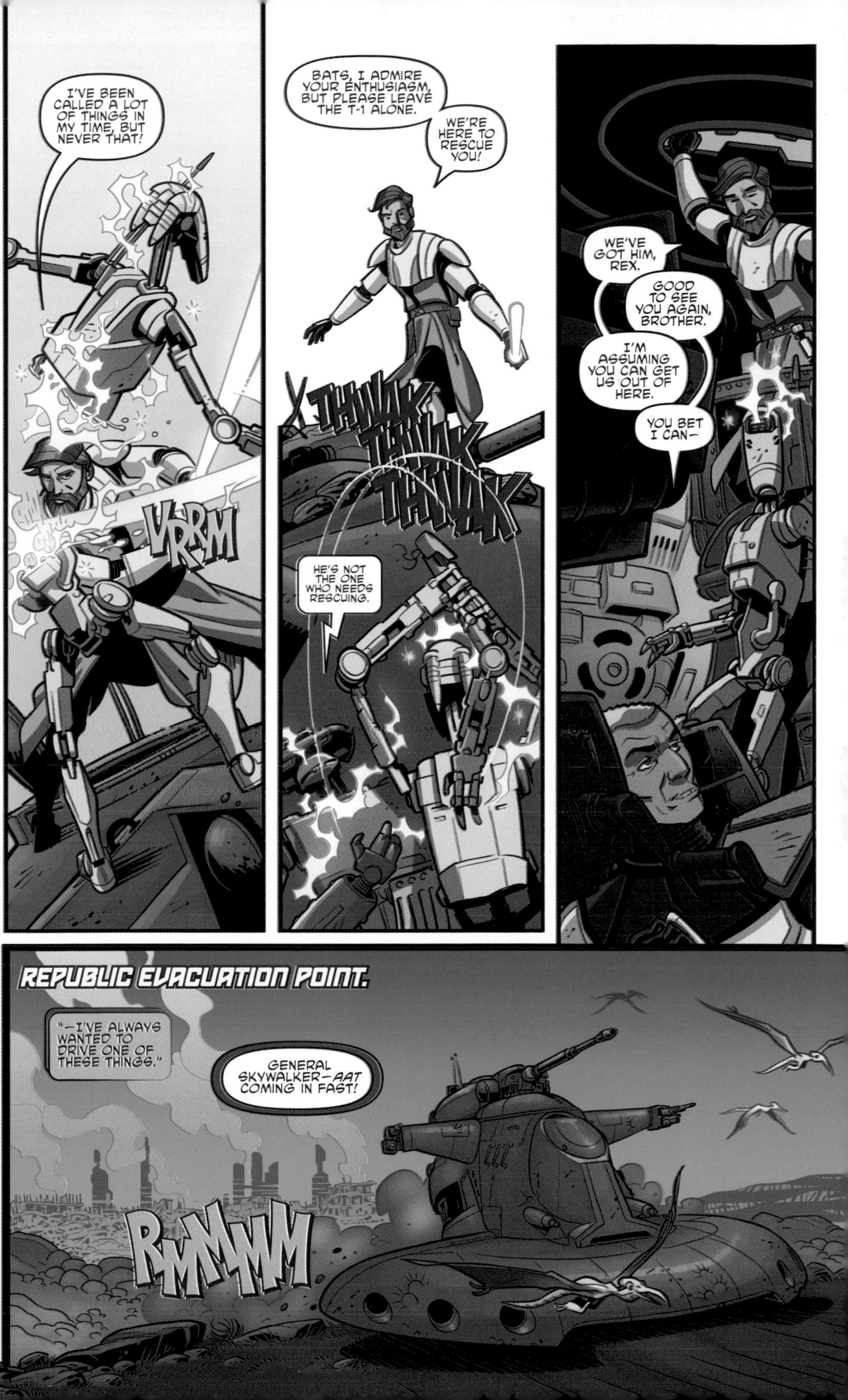
I'VE BEEN CALLED A LOT OF THINGS IN MY TIME, BUT NEVER THAT!
VRRM
BATS, I ADMIRE YOUR ENTHUSIASM, BUT PLEASE LEAVE THE T-1 ALONE.
WE'RE HERE TO RESCUE YOU!
THWAK THWAK THWAK
HE'S NOT THE ONE WHO NEEDS RESCUING.
WE'VE GOT HIM, REX.
GOOD TO SEE YOU AGAIN, BROTHER.
I'M ASSUMING YOU CAN GET US OUT OF HERE.
YOU BET I CAN—
REPUBLIC EVACUATION POINT.
"—I'VE ALWAYS WANTED TO DRIVE ONE OF THESE THINGS."
GENERAL SKYWALKER—AAT COMING IN FAST!
RMMMMM

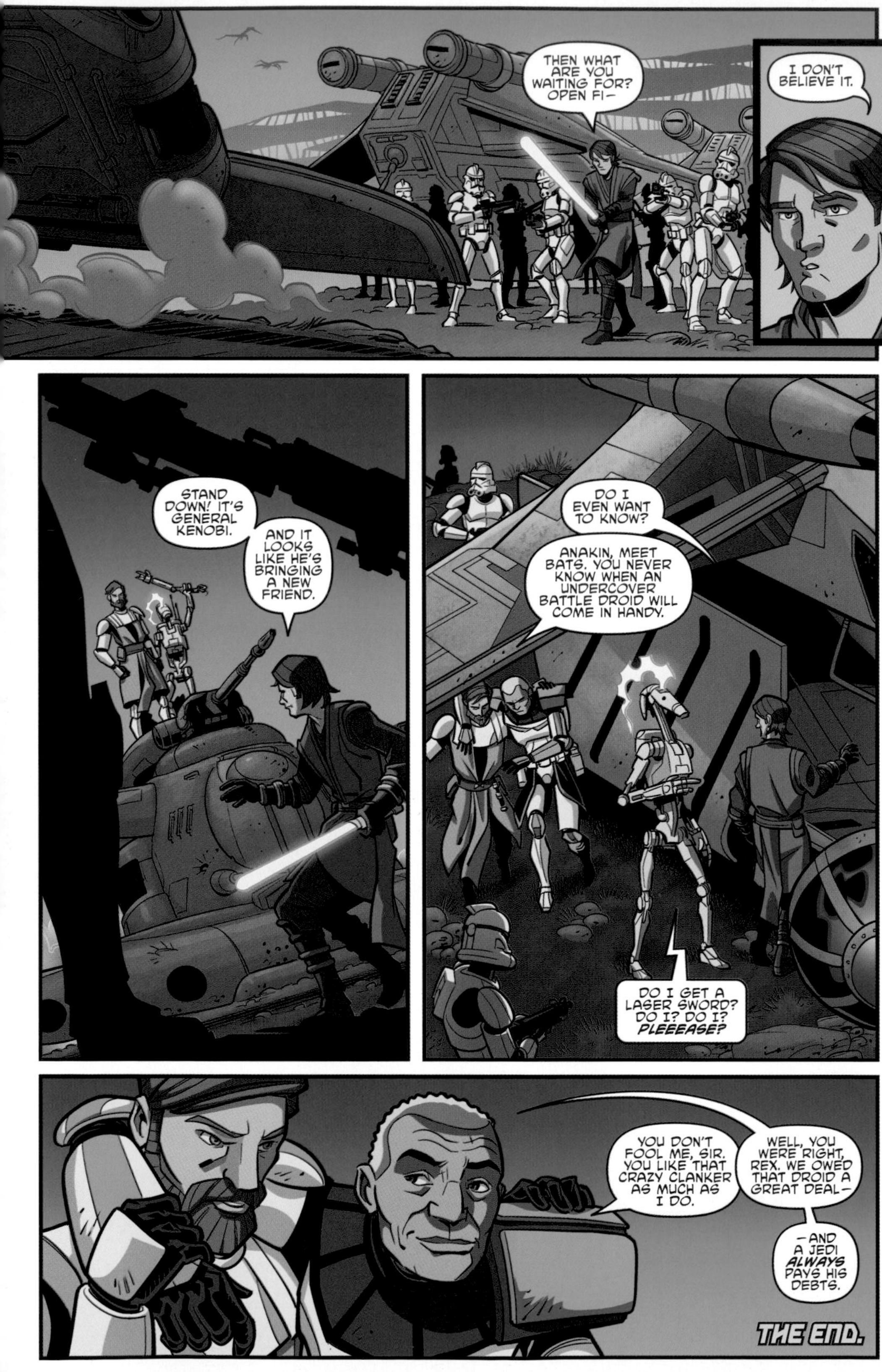
THEN WHAT ARE YOU WAITING FOR? OPEN FI—
I DON'T BELIEVE IT.
STAND DOWN! IT'S GENERAL KENOBI.
AND IT LOOKS LIKE HE'S BRINGING A NEW FRIEND.
DO I EVEN WANT TO KNOW?
ANAKIN, MEET BATS. YOU NEVER KNOW WHEN AN UNDERCOVER BATTLE DROID WILL COME IN HANDY.
DO I GET A LASER SWORD? DO I? DO I? PLEEEASE?
WELL, YOU WERE RIGHT, REX. WE OWED THAT DROID A GREAT DEAL—
YOU DON'T FOOL ME, SIR. YOU LIKE THAT CRAZY CLANKER AS MUCH AS I DO.
—AND A JEDI ALWAYS PAYS HIS DEBTS.
THE END.

STAR WARS
ADVENTURES

Hide and Seek

WRITER
CAVAN SCOTT

ARTIST & COLORIST
DEREK CHARM

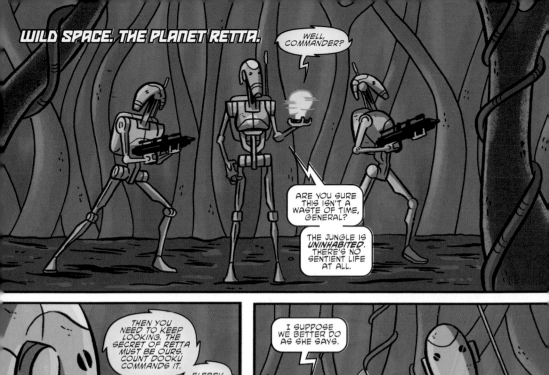

WILD SPACE. THE PLANET RETTA.
WELL, COMMANDER?
ARE YOU SURE THIS ISN'T A WASTE OF TIME, GENERAL?
THE JUNGLE IS UNINHABITED. THERE'S NO SENTIENT LIFE AT ALL.
THEN YOU NEED TO KEEP LOOKING. THE SECRET OF RETTA MUST BE OURS. COUNT DOOKU COMMANDS IT.
FLEBEK OUT.
VZZT
WELL, THERE'S NO NEED TO SNAP.
I SUPPOSE WE BETTER DO AS SHE SAYS.
RUSTLE
COMMANDER, I THINK I'VE FOUND SOMETHING.
VMMM
OH, YOU'VE FOUND SOMETHING ALL RIGHT—

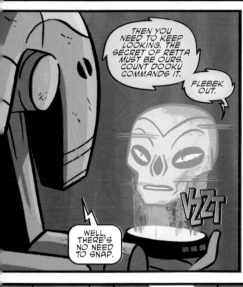

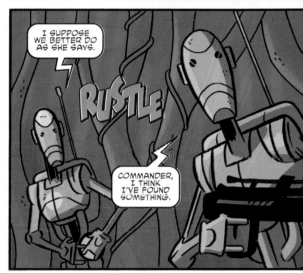

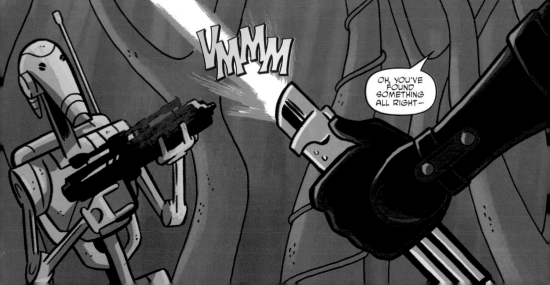

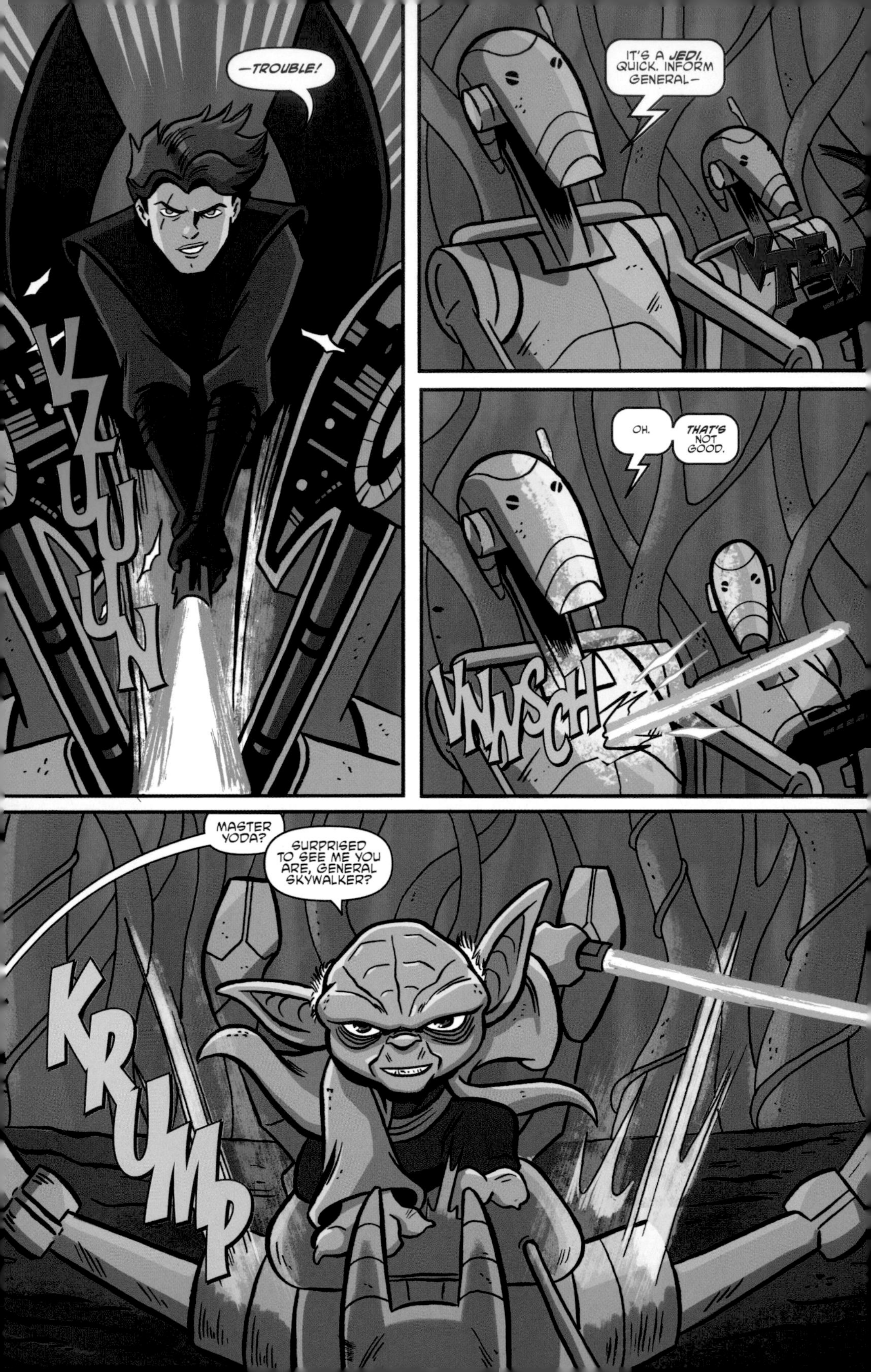
—TROUBLE!
KZUUUN
IT'S A JEDI. QUICK. INFORM GENERAL—
VTEW
OH.
THAT'S NOT GOOD.
VNNSCH
MASTER YODA?
SURPRISED TO SEE ME YOU ARE, GENERAL SKYWALKER?
KRUMP

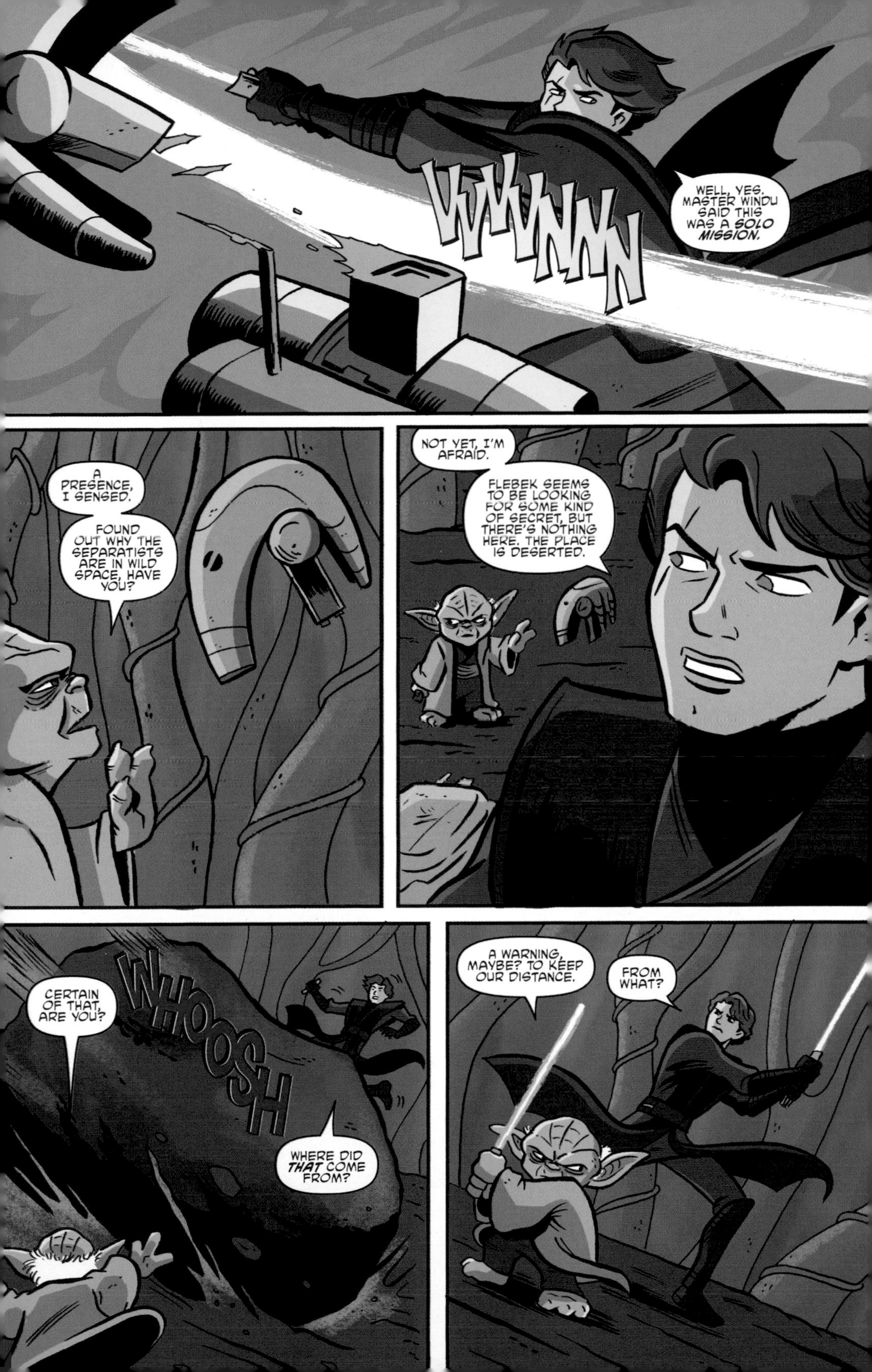
VVVVNNNN
WELL, YES. MASTER WINDU SAID THIS WAS A *SOLO MISSION.*
A PRESENCE, I SENSED.
FOUND OUT WHY THE SEPARATISTS ARE IN WILD SPACE, HAVE YOU?
NOT YET, I'M AFRAID.
FLEBEK SEEMS TO BE LOOKING FOR SOME KIND OF SECRET, BUT THERE'S NOTHING HERE. THE PLACE IS DESERTED.
CERTAIN OF THAT, ARE YOU?
WHOOSH
WHERE DID *THAT* COME FROM?
A WARNING, MAYBE? TO KEEP OUR DISTANCE.
FROM WHAT?

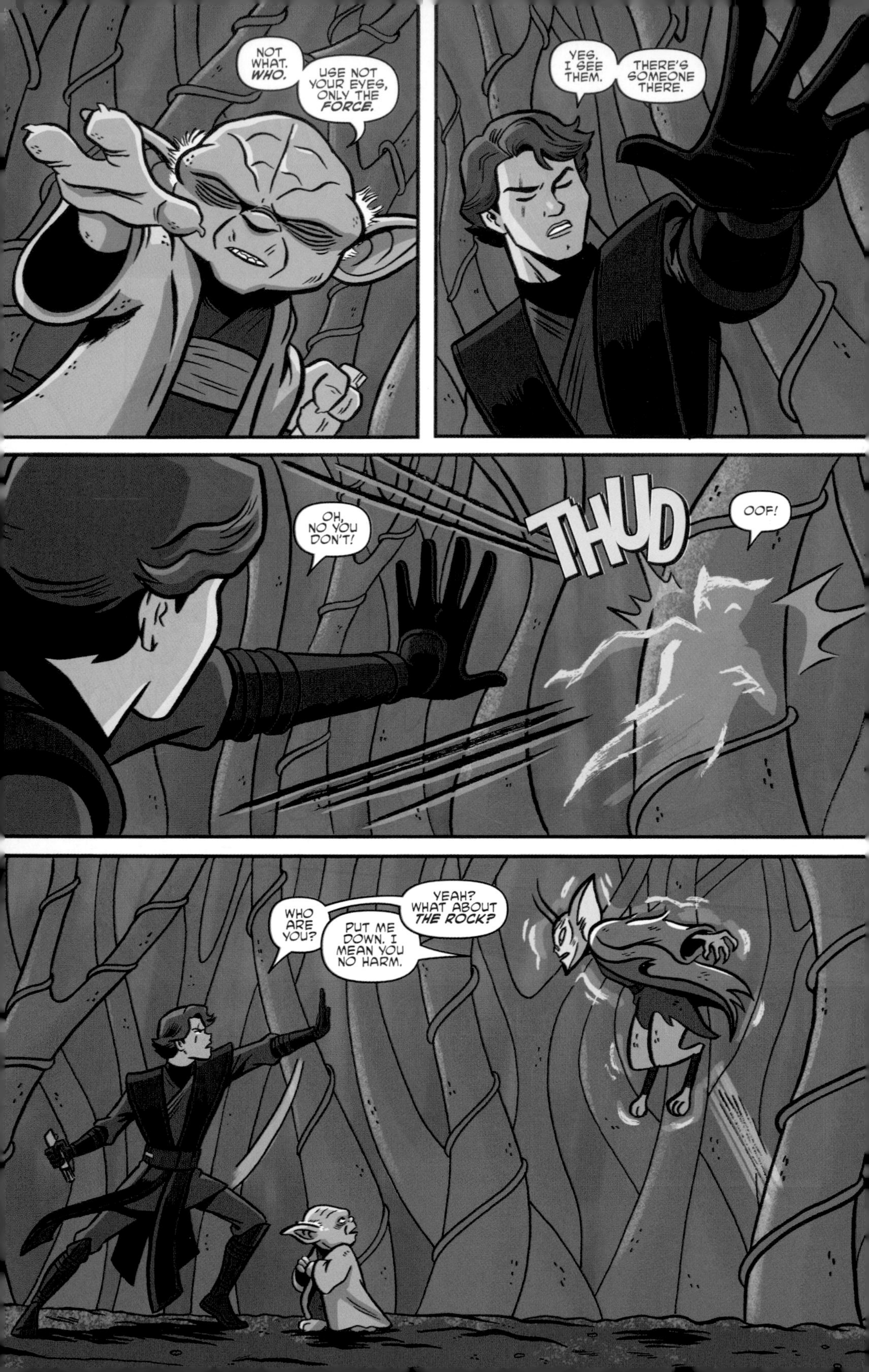
NOT WHAT. WHO.
USE NOT YOUR EYES, ONLY THE FORCE.
YES. I SEE THEM.
THERE'S SOMEONE THERE.
OH, NO YOU DON'T!
THUD
OOF!
WHO ARE YOU?
PUT ME DOWN. I MEAN YOU NO HARM.
YEAH? WHAT ABOUT THE ROCK?

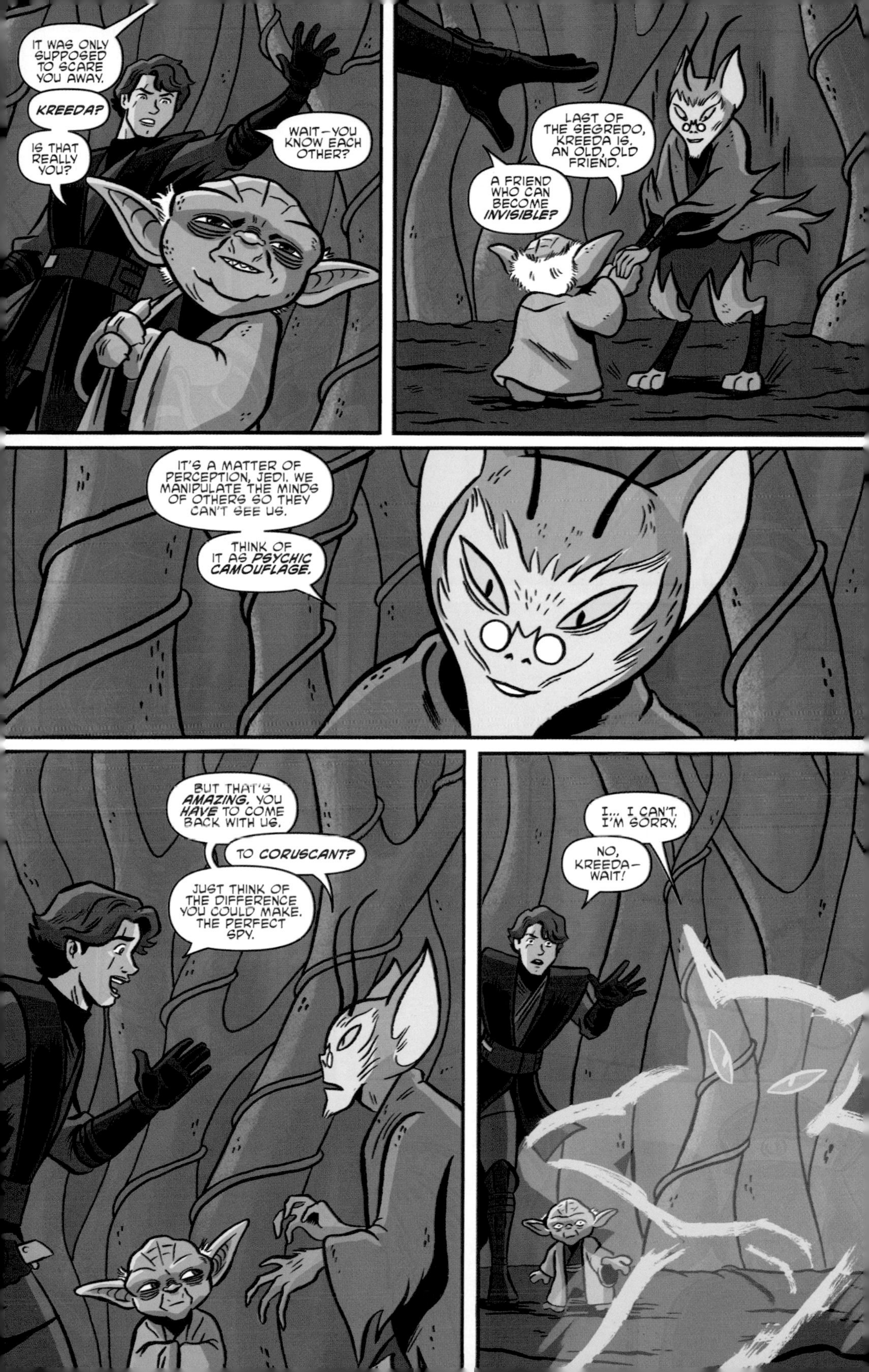
IT WAS ONLY SUPPOSED TO SCARE YOU AWAY.
KREEDA?
IS THAT REALLY YOU?
WAIT—YOU KNOW EACH OTHER?
LAST OF THE SEGREDO, KREEDA IS. AN OLD, OLD FRIEND.
A FRIEND WHO CAN BECOME INVISIBLE?
IT'S A MATTER OF PERCEPTION, JEDI. WE MANIPULATE THE MINDS OF OTHERS SO THEY CAN'T SEE US.
THINK OF IT AS PSYCHIC CAMOUFLAGE.
BUT THAT'S AMAZING. YOU HAVE TO COME BACK WITH US.
TO CORUSCANT?
JUST THINK OF THE DIFFERENCE YOU COULD MAKE. THE PERFECT SPY.
I... I CAN'T. I'M SORRY.
NO, KREEDA—WAIT!

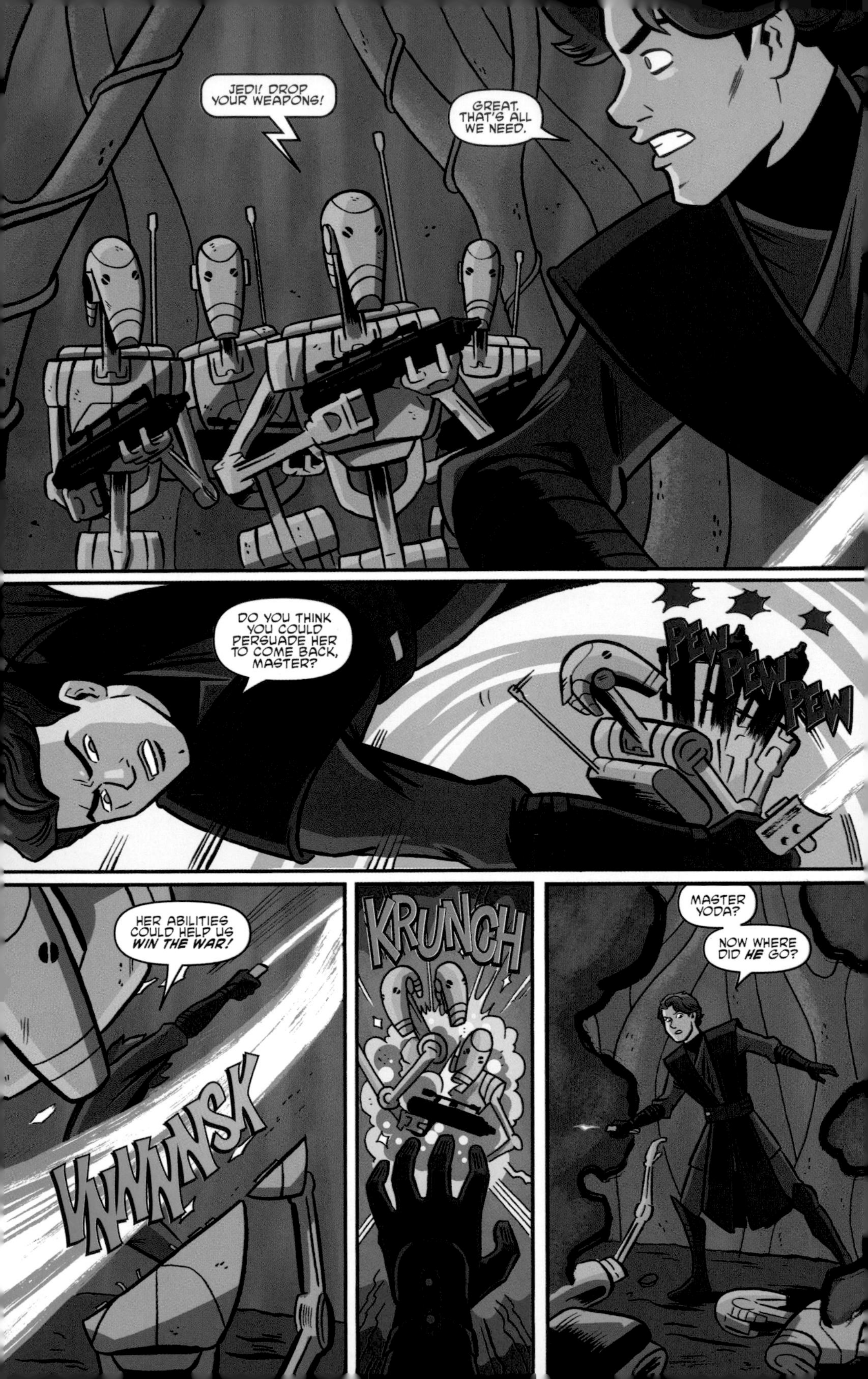
JEDI! DROP YOUR WEAPONS!
GREAT. THAT'S ALL WE NEED.
DO YOU THINK YOU COULD PERSUADE HER TO COME BACK, MASTER?
PEW PEW PEW
HER ABILITIES COULD HELP US *WIN THE WAR!*
VWWNSK
KRUNCH
MASTER YODA?
NOW WHERE DID *HE* GO?

"I WISH EVERYONE WOULD STOP *DISAPPEARING!*"

KREEDA?

SHOW YOURSELF. TALK WE MUST.

HMM!

FROM WHERE DID YOU COME?

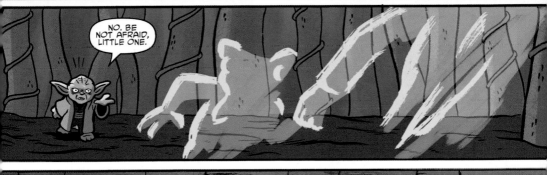

NO. BE NOT AFRAID, LITTLE ONE.

HMM.

WHAT ARE YOU UP TO, KREEDA, OLD FRIEND?

WHAT ARE YOU HIDING?

AAAH...

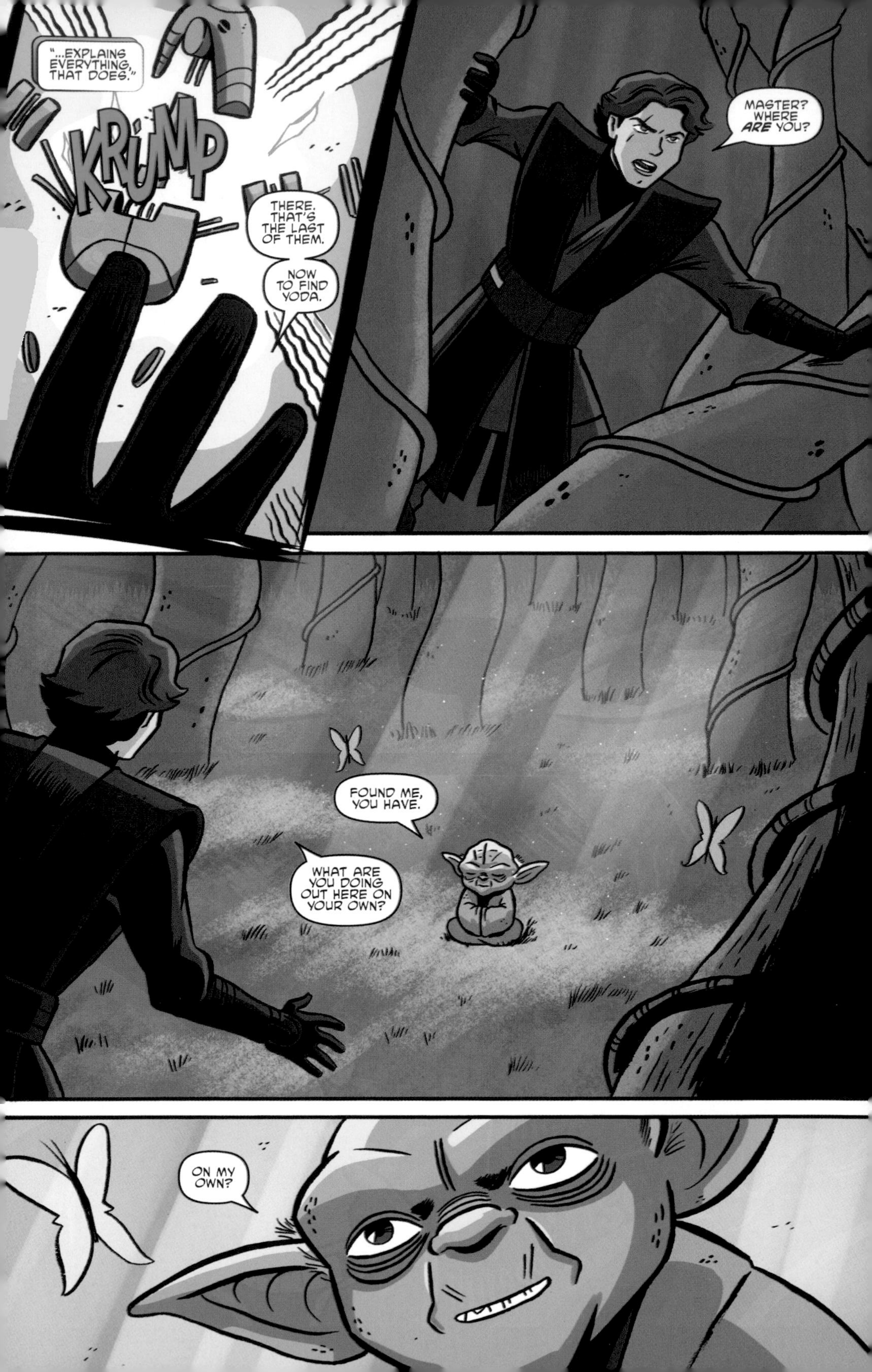
"...EXPLAINS EVERYTHING, THAT DOES."
KRUMP
THERE. THAT'S THE LAST OF THEM.
NOW TO FIND YODA.
MASTER? WHERE ARE YOU?
FOUND ME, YOU HAVE.
WHAT ARE YOU DOING OUT HERE ON YOUR OWN?
ON MY OWN?

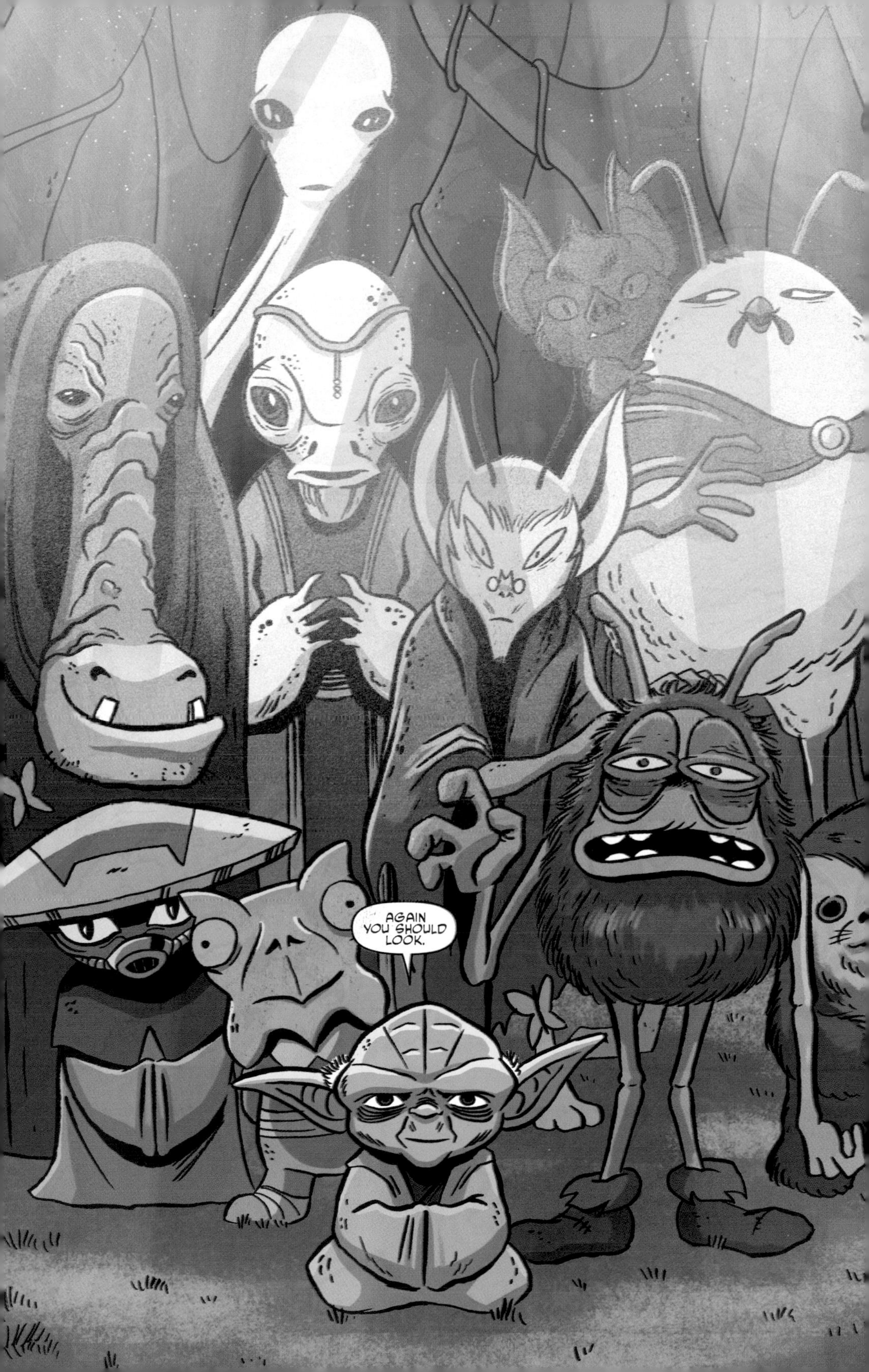
AGAIN YOU SHOULD LOOK.

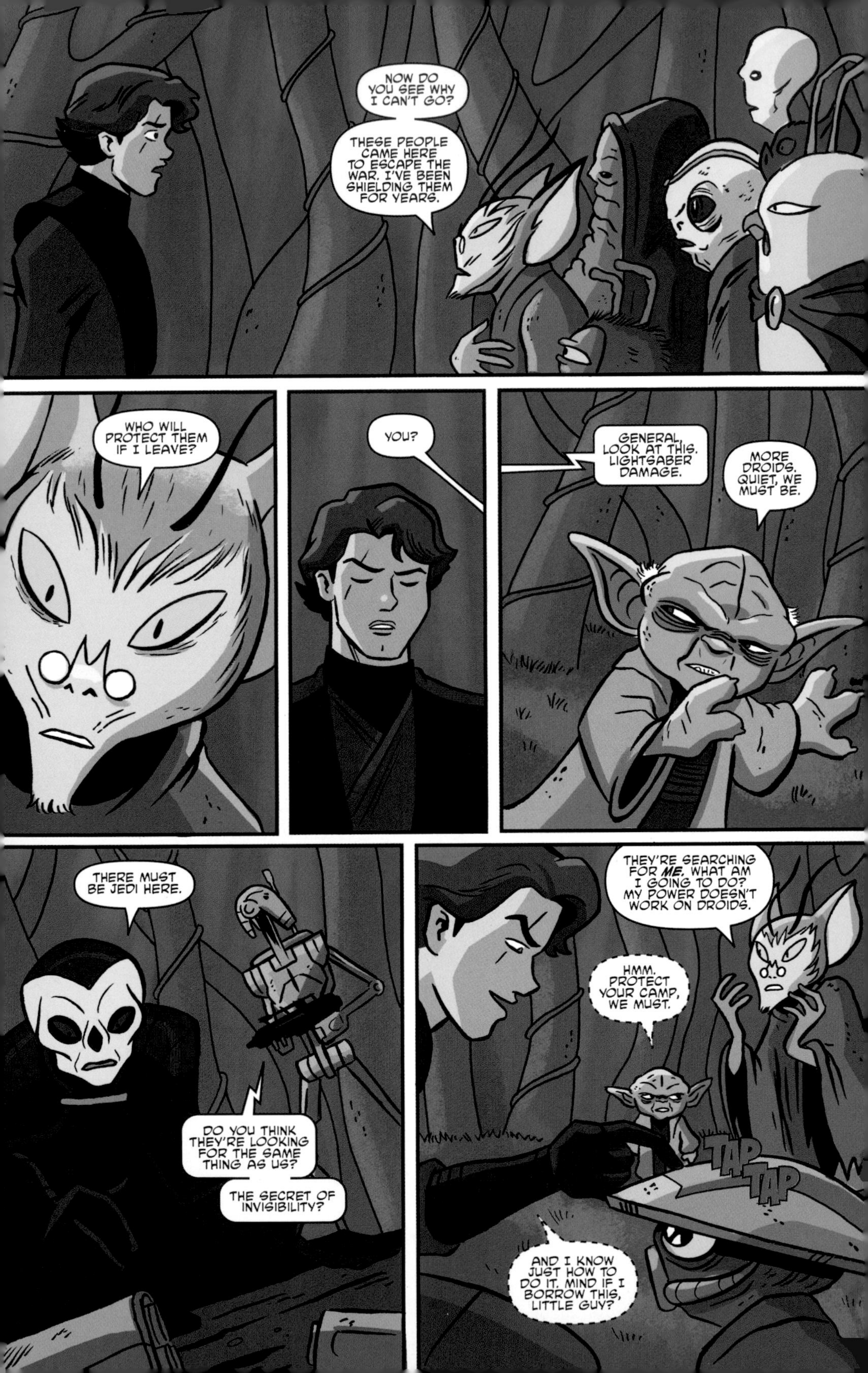
NOW DO YOU SEE WHY I CAN'T GO?
THESE PEOPLE CAME HERE TO ESCAPE THE WAR. I'VE BEEN SHIELDING THEM FOR YEARS.
WHO WILL PROTECT THEM IF I LEAVE?
YOU?
GENERAL, LOOK AT THIS. LIGHTSABER DAMAGE.
MORE DROIDS. QUIET, WE MUST BE.
THERE MUST BE JEDI HERE.
DO YOU THINK THEY'RE LOOKING FOR THE SAME THING AS US?
THE SECRET OF INVISIBILITY?
THEY'RE SEARCHING FOR *ME*. WHAT AM I GOING TO DO? MY POWER DOESN'T WORK ON DROIDS.
HMM. PROTECT YOUR CAMP, WE MUST.
TAP TAP
AND I KNOW JUST HOW TO DO IT. MIND IF I BORROW THIS, LITTLE GUY?

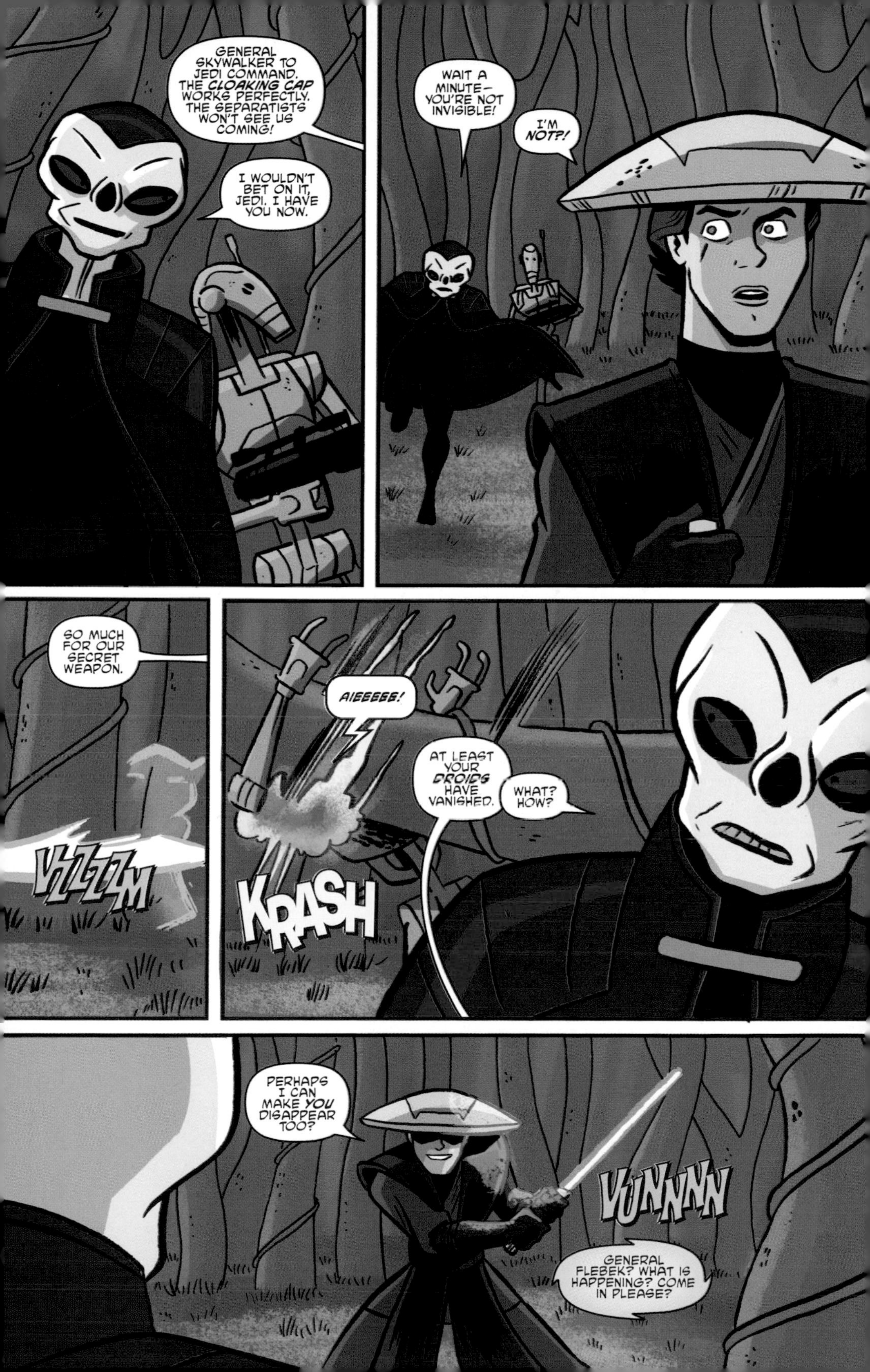
GENERAL SKYWALKER TO JEDI COMMAND. THE CLOAKING CAP WORKS PERFECTLY. THE SEPARATISTS WON'T SEE US COMING!
I WOULDN'T BET ON IT, JEDI. I HAVE YOU NOW.
WAIT A MINUTE— YOU'RE NOT INVISIBLE!
I'M NOT?!
SO MUCH FOR OUR SECRET WEAPON.
VZZZZM
AIEEEEE!
AT LEAST YOUR DROIDS HAVE VANISHED.
WHAT? HOW?
KRASH
PERHAPS I CAN MAKE YOU DISAPPEAR TOO?
VUNNNN
GENERAL FLEBEK? WHAT IS HAPPENING? COME IN PLEASE?

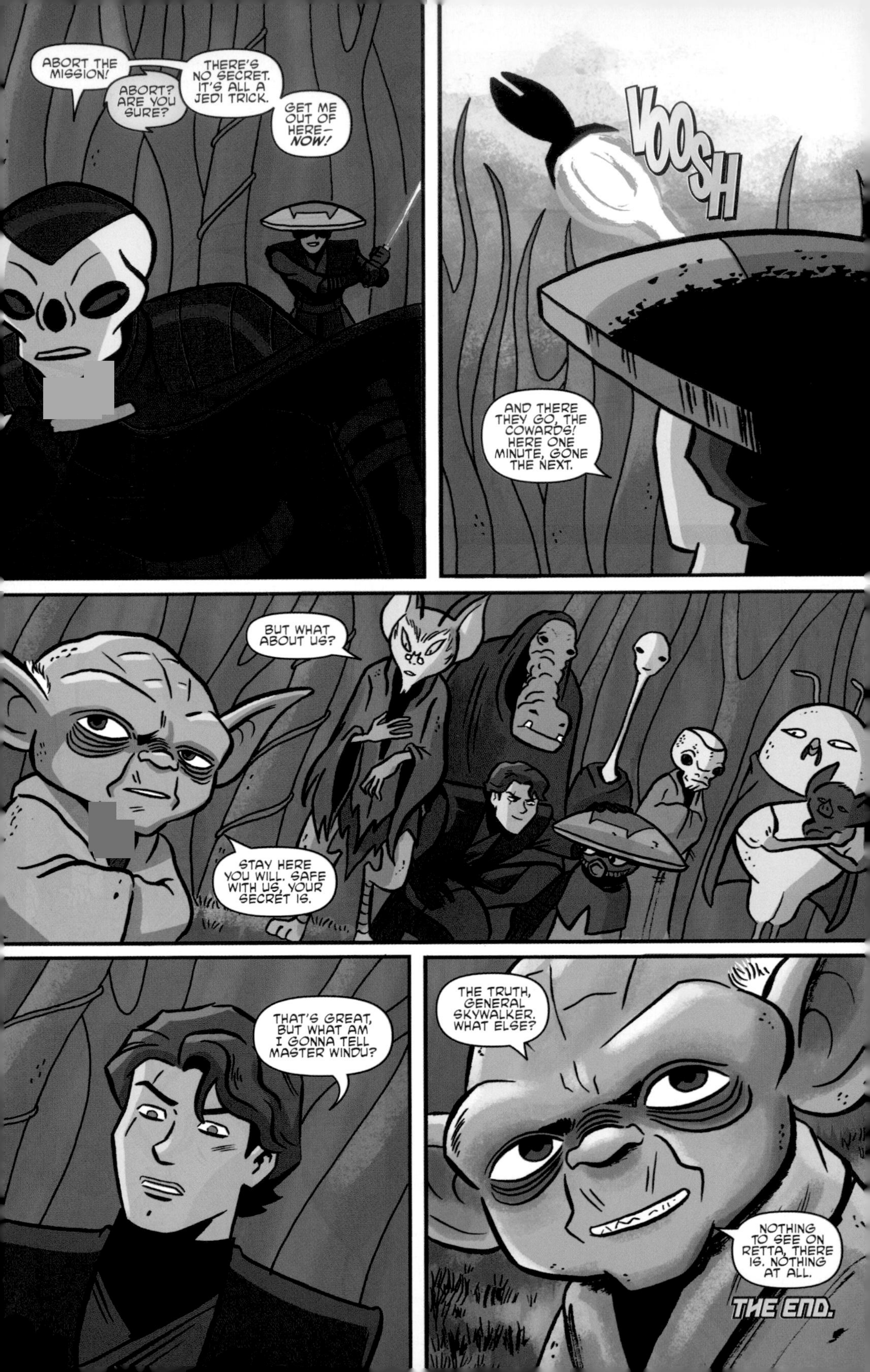
ABORT THE MISSION!
ABORT? ARE YOU SURE?
THERE'S NO SECRET. IT'S ALL A JEDI TRICK.
GET ME OUT OF HERE– NOW!
VOOSH
AND THERE THEY GO, THE COWARDS! HERE ONE MINUTE, GONE THE NEXT.
BUT WHAT ABOUT US?
STAY HERE YOU WILL. SAFE WITH US, YOUR SECRET IS.
THAT'S GREAT, BUT WHAT AM I GONNA TELL MASTER WINDU?
THE TRUTH, GENERAL SKYWALKER. WHAT ELSE?
NOTHING TO SEE ON RETTA, THERE IS. NOTHING AT ALL.
THE END.

THE BIG MARCH

WRITER ARTIST & COLORIST
NICK BROKENSHIRE

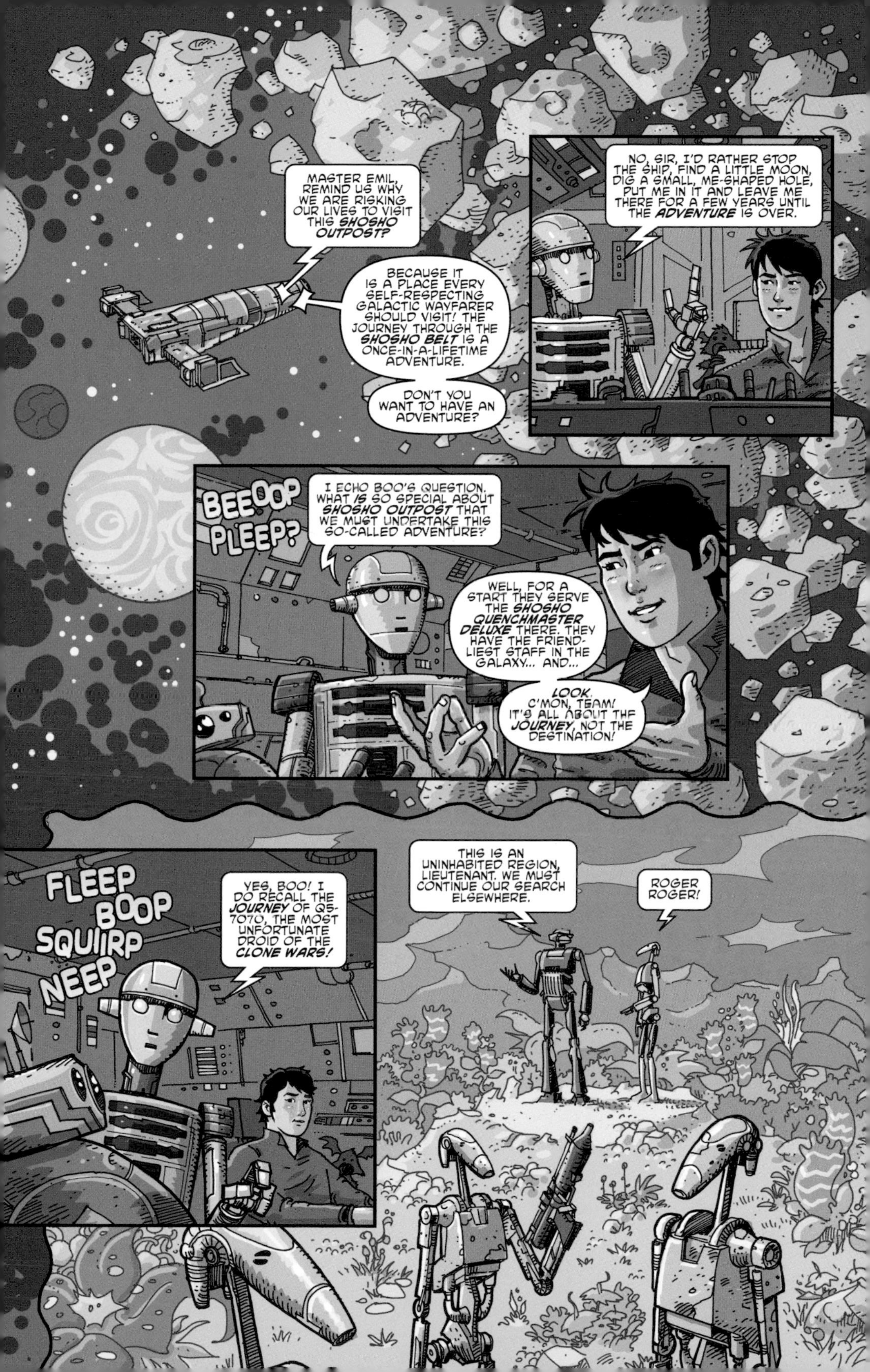

MASTER EMIL, REMIND US WHY WE ARE RISKING OUR LIVES TO VISIT THIS SHOSHO OUTPOST?
BECAUSE IT IS A PLACE EVERY SELF-RESPECTING GALACTIC WAYFARER SHOULD VISIT! THE JOURNEY THROUGH THE SHOSHO BELT IS A ONCE-IN-A-LIFETIME ADVENTURE.
DON'T YOU WANT TO HAVE AN ADVENTURE?
NO, SIR, I'D RATHER STOP THE SHIP, FIND A LITTLE MOON, DIG A SMALL, ME-SHAPED HOLE, PUT ME IN IT AND LEAVE ME THERE FOR A FEW YEARS UNTIL THE ADVENTURE IS OVER.
BEEOOP PLEEP?
I ECHO BOO'S QUESTION. WHAT IS SO SPECIAL ABOUT SHOSHO OUTPOST THAT WE MUST UNDERTAKE THIS SO-CALLED ADVENTURE?
WELL, FOR A START THEY SERVE THE SHOSHO QUENCHMASTER DELUXE THERE. THEY HAVE THE FRIENDLIEST STAFF IN THE GALAXY... AND...
LOOK. C'MON, TEAM! IT'S ALL ABOUT THE JOURNEY, NOT THE DESTINATION!
FLEEP BOOP SQUIIRP NEEP
YES, BOO! I DO RECALL THE JOURNEY OF QS-7070, THE MOST UNFORTUNATE DROID OF THE CLONE WARS!
THIS IS AN UNINHABITED REGION, LIEUTENANT. WE MUST CONTINUE OUR SEARCH ELSEWHERE.
ROGER ROGER!

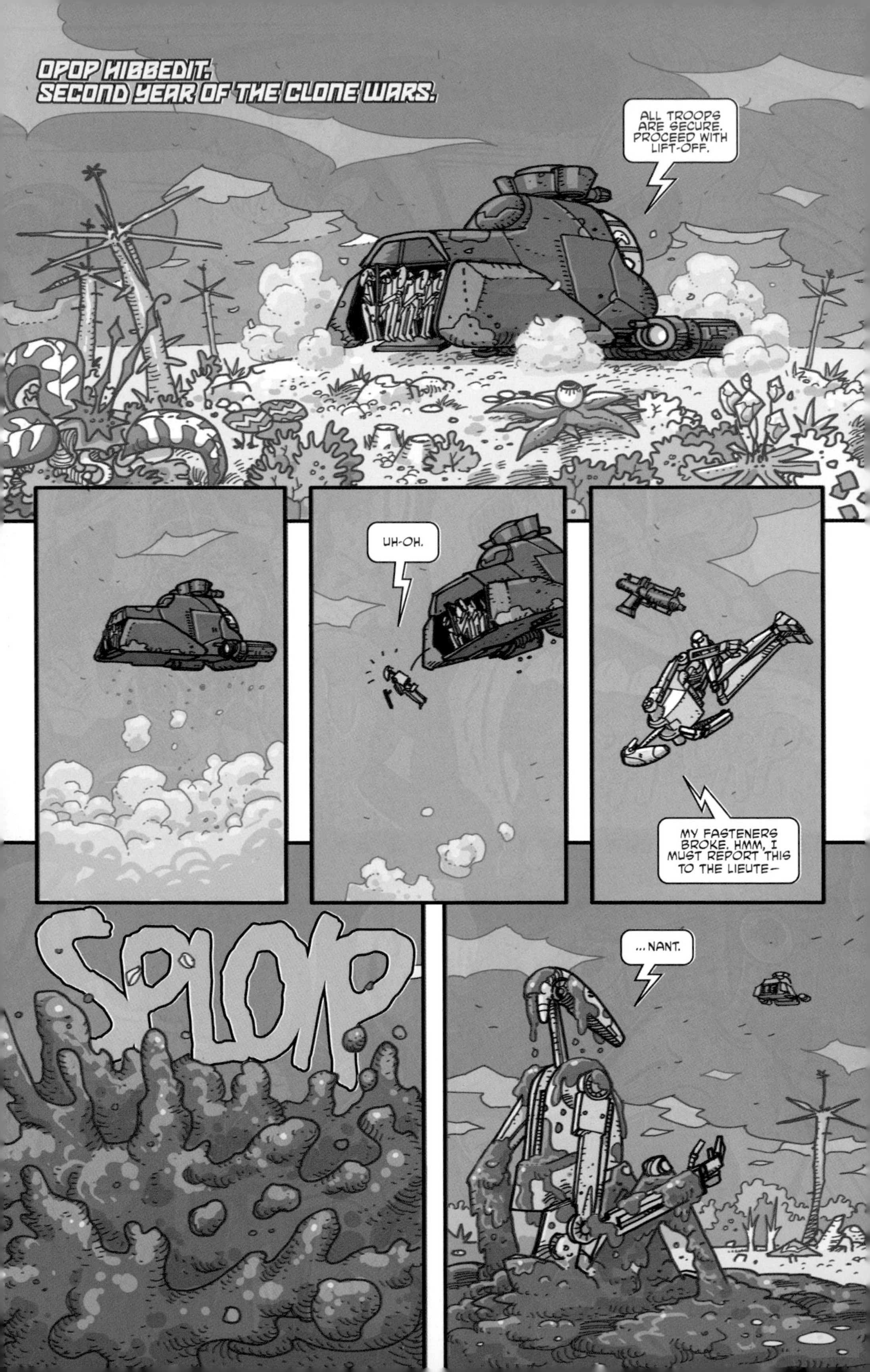
OPOP HIBBEDIT.
SECOND YEAR OF THE CLONE WARS.
ALL TROOPS ARE SECURE. PROCEED WITH LIFT-OFF.
UH-OH.
MY FASTENERS BROKE. HMM, I MUST REPORT THIS TO THE LIEUTE—
SPLOP
...NANT.

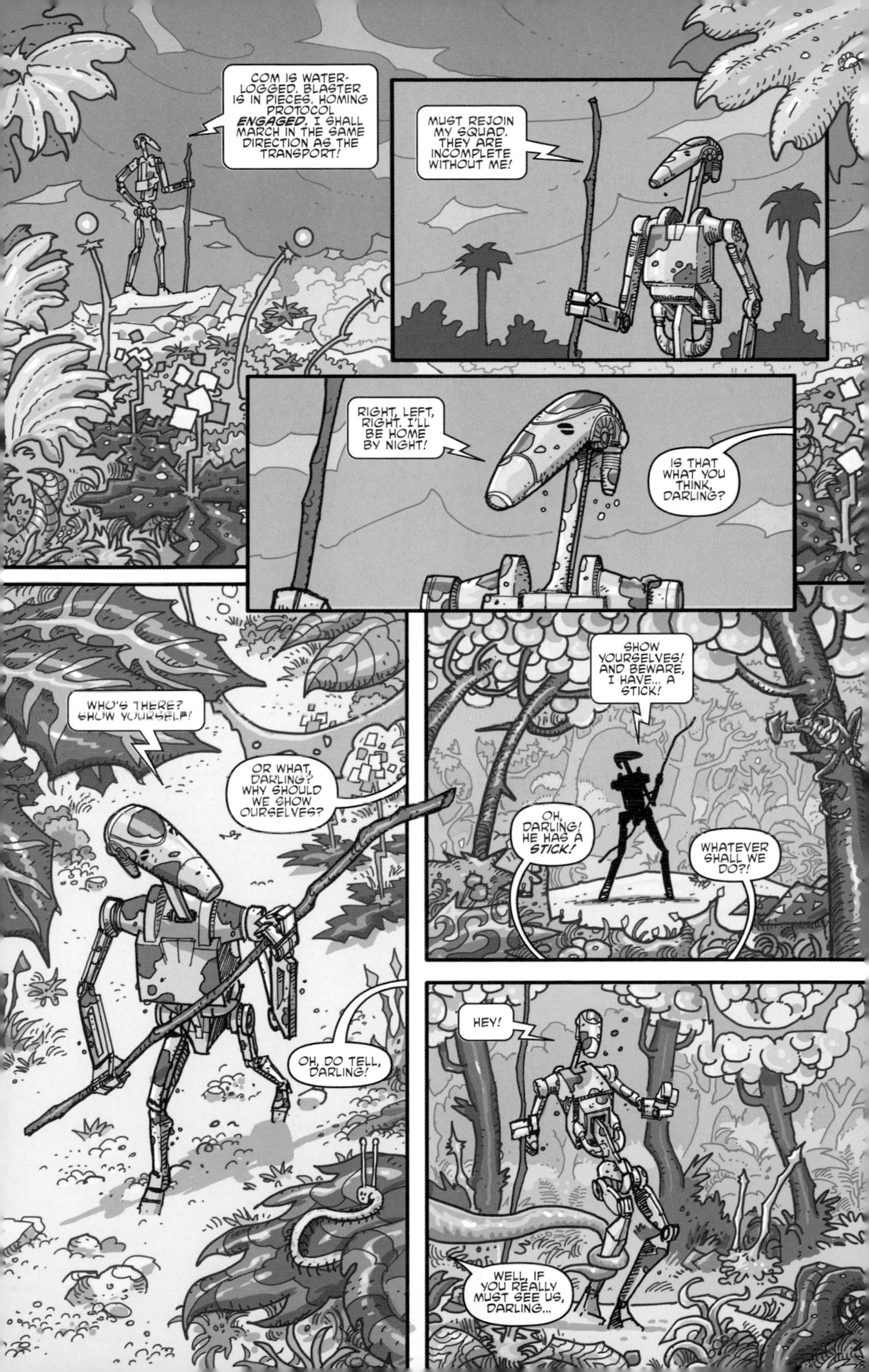
COM IS WATER-LOGGED. BLASTER IS IN PIECES. HOMING PROTOCOL **ENGAGED.** I SHALL MARCH IN THE SAME DIRECTION AS THE TRANSPORT!
MUST REJOIN MY SQUAD. THEY ARE INCOMPLETE WITHOUT ME!
RIGHT, LEFT, RIGHT. I'LL BE HOME BY NIGHT!
IS THAT WHAT YOU THINK, DARLING?
WHO'S THERE? SHOW YOURSELF!
OR WHAT, DARLING? WHY SHOULD WE SHOW OURSELVES?
OH, DO TELL, DARLING!
SHOW YOURSELVES! AND BEWARE, I HAVE... A STICK!
OH, DARLING! HE HAS A ***STICK!***
WHATEVER SHALL WE DO?!
HEY!
WELL, IF YOU REALLY MUST SEE US, DARLING...

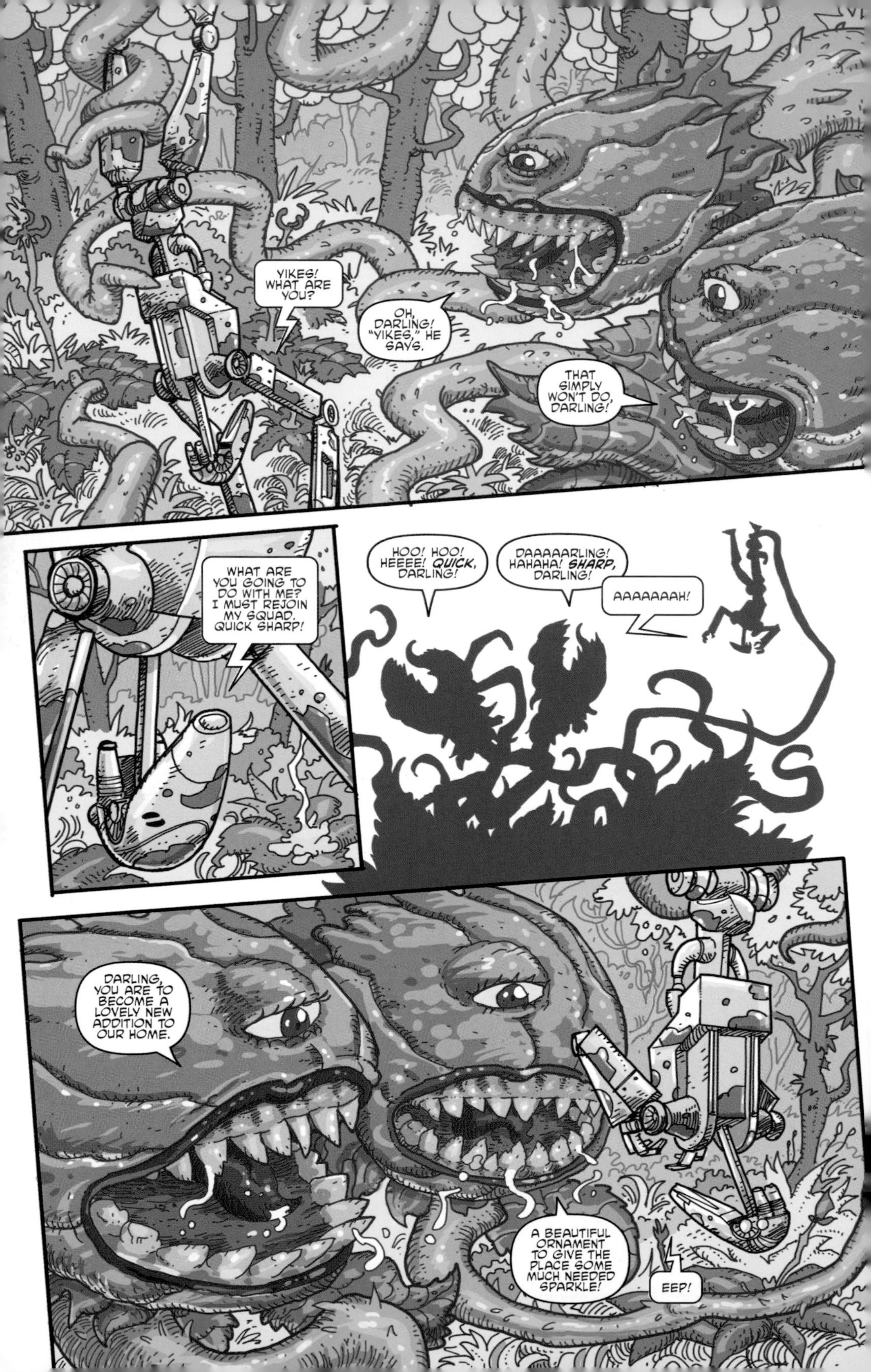
YIKES! WHAT ARE YOU?
OH, DARLING! "YIKES," HE SAYS.
THAT SIMPLY WON'T DO, DARLING!
WHAT ARE YOU GOING TO DO WITH ME? I MUST REJOIN MY SQUAD. QUICK SHARP!
HOO! HOO! HEEEE! QUICK, DARLING!
DAAAAARLING! HAHAHA! SHARP, DARLING!
AAAAAAAH!
DARLING, YOU ARE TO BECOME A LOVELY NEW ADDITION TO OUR HOME.
A BEAUTIFUL ORNAMENT TO GIVE THE PLACE SOME MUCH NEEDED SPARKLE!
EEP!

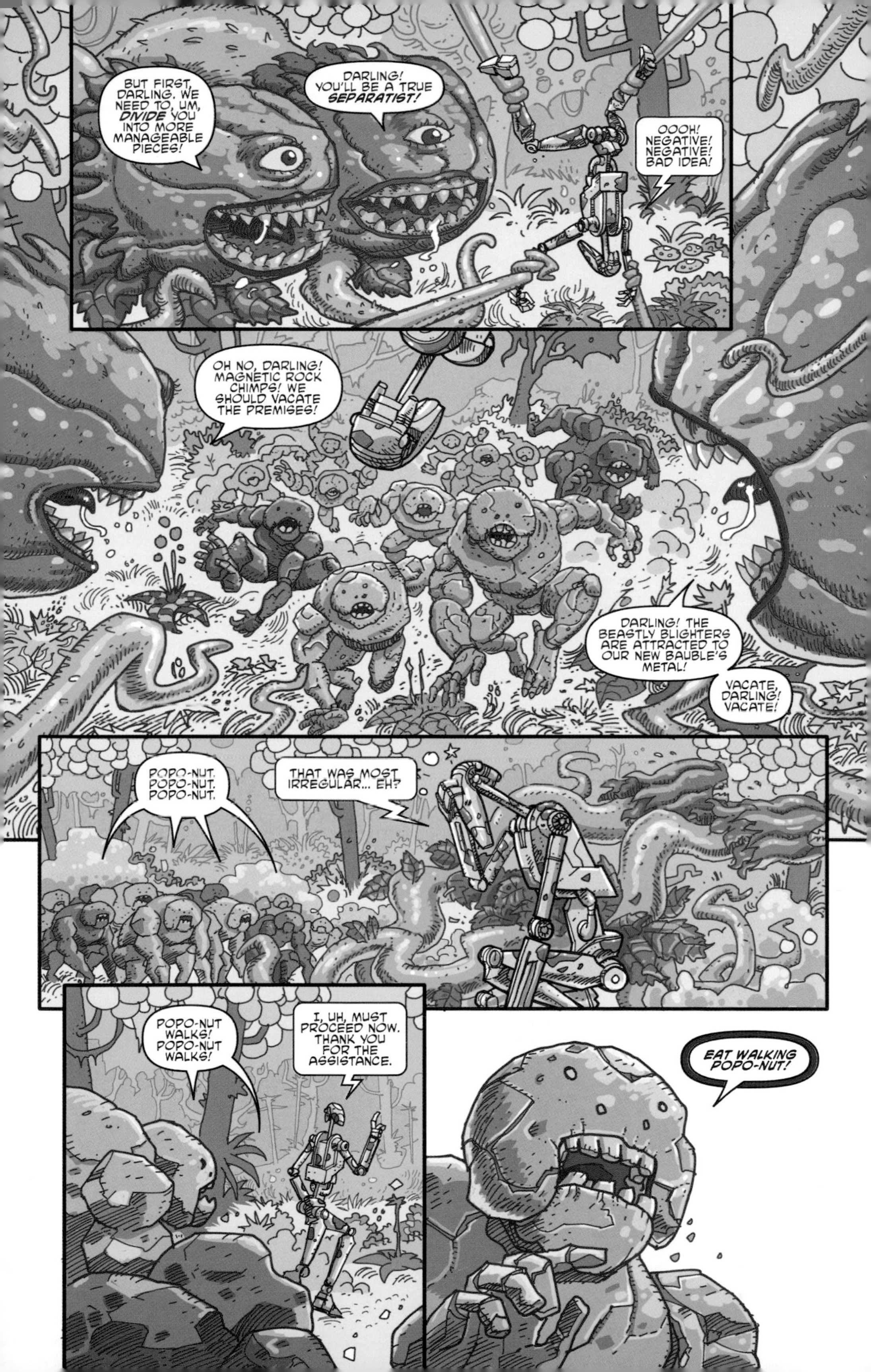
BUT FIRST, DARLING. WE NEED TO, UM, DIVIDE YOU INTO MORE MANAGEABLE PIECES!
DARLING! YOU'LL BE A TRUE SEPARATIST!
OOOH! NEGATIVE! NEGATIVE! BAD IDEA!
OH NO, DARLING! MAGNETIC ROCK CHIMPS! WE SHOULD VACATE THE PREMISES!
DARLING! THE BEASTLY BLIGHTERS ARE ATTRACTED TO OUR NEW BAUBLE'S METAL!
VACATE, DARLING! VACATE!
POPO-NUT. POPO-NUT. POPO-NUT.
THAT WAS MOST IRREGULAR... EH?
POPO-NUT WALKS! POPO-NUT WALKS!
I, UH, MUST PROCEED NOW. THANK YOU FOR THE ASSISTANCE.
EAT WALKING POPO-NUT!

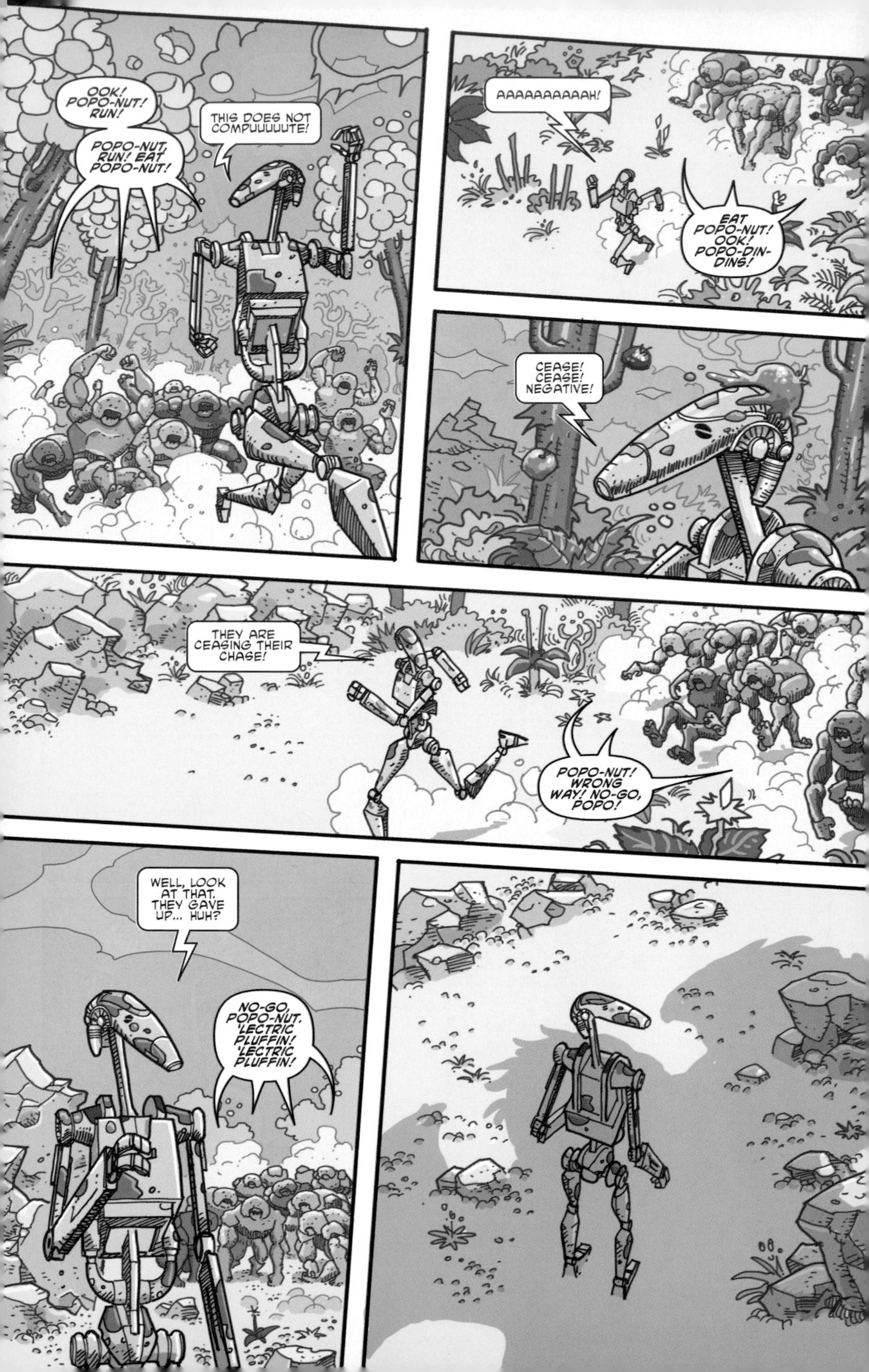
OOK! POPO-NUT! RUN!
POPO-NUT, RUN! EAT POPO-NUT!
THIS DOES NOT COMPUUUUUTE!
AAAAAAAAAAH!
EAT POPO-NUT! OOK! POPO-DIN-DINS!
CEASE! CEASE! NEGATIVE!
THEY ARE CEASING THEIR CHASE!
POPO-NUT! WRONG WAY! NO-GO, POPO!
WELL, LOOK AT THAT. THEY GAVE UP... HUH?
NO-GO, POPO-NUT. 'LECTRIC PLUFFIN! 'LECTRIC PLUFFIN!

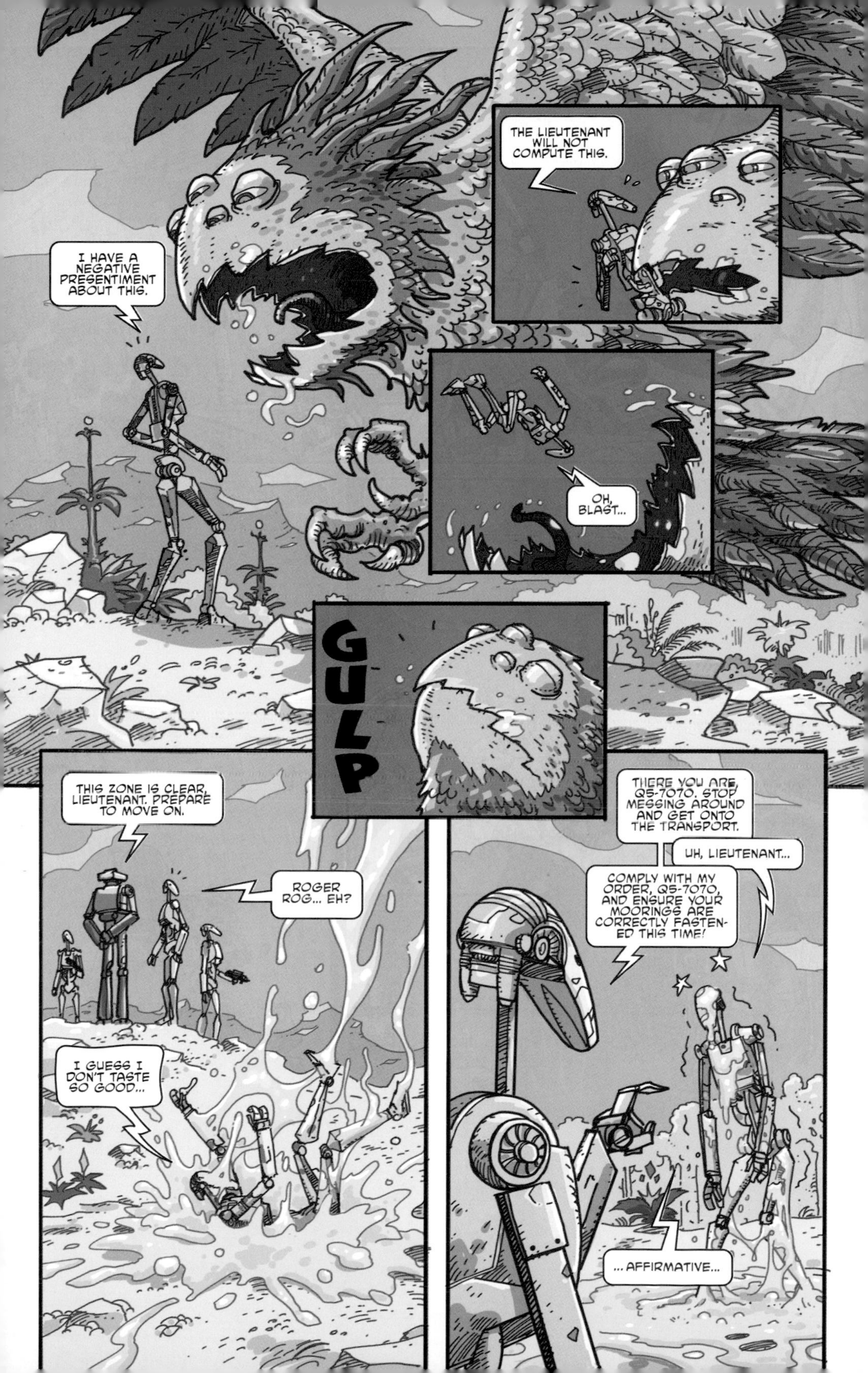

I HAVE A NEGATIVE PRESENTIMENT ABOUT THIS.
THE LIEUTENANT WILL NOT COMPUTE THIS.
OH, BLAST...
GULP
THIS ZONE IS CLEAR, LIEUTENANT. PREPARE TO MOVE ON.
ROGER ROG... EH?
I GUESS I DON'T TASTE SO GOOD...
THERE YOU ARE, Q5-7070. STOP MESSING AROUND AND GET ONTO THE TRANSPORT.
UH, LIEUTENANT...
COMPLY WITH MY ORDER, Q5-7070, AND ENSURE YOUR MOORINGS ARE CORRECTLY FASTEN-ED THIS TIME!
...AFFIRMATIVE...

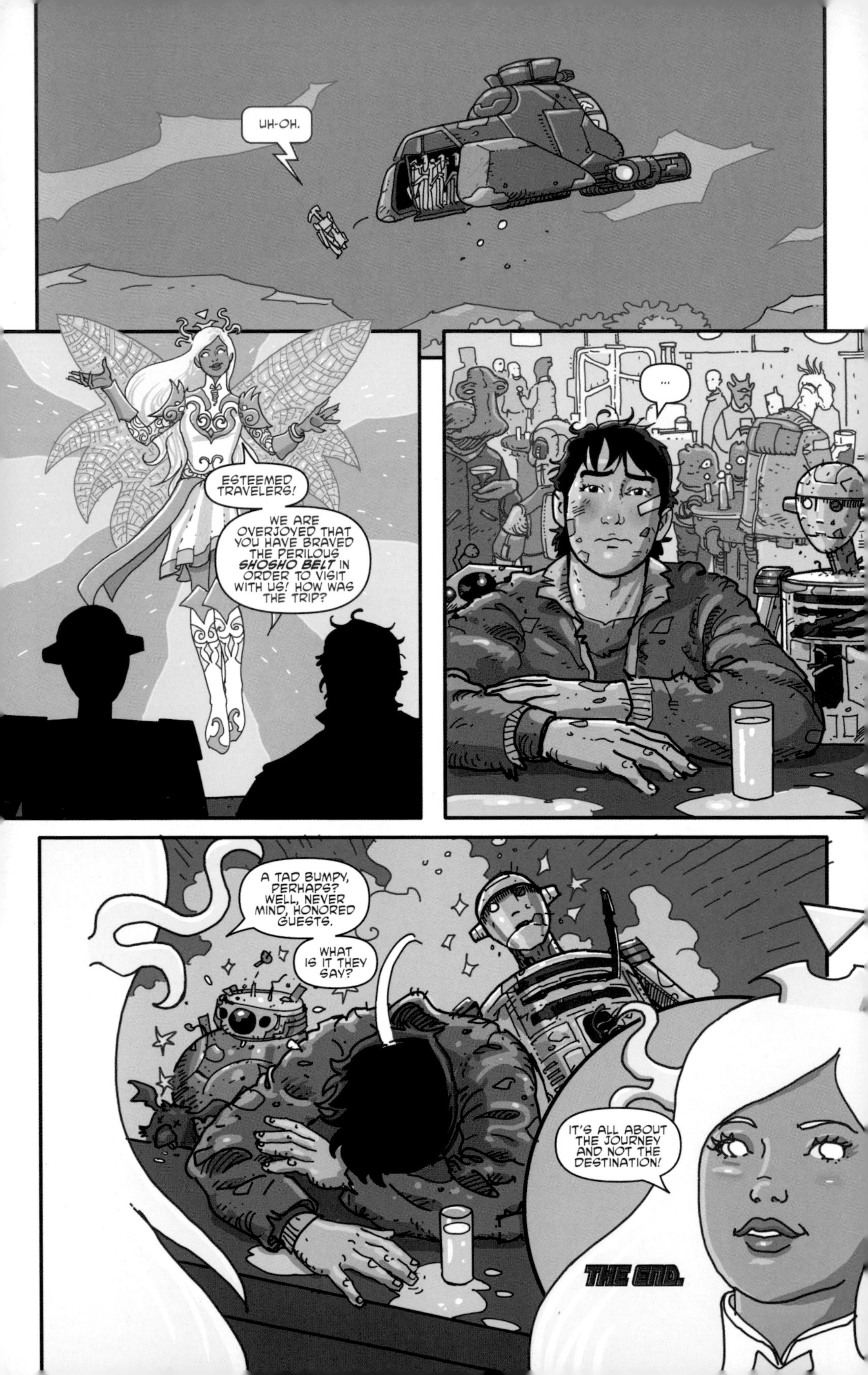
UH-OH.
ESTEEMED TRAVELERS!
WE ARE OVERJOYED THAT YOU HAVE BRAVED THE PERILOUS SHOSHO BELT IN ORDER TO VISIT WITH US! HOW WAS THE TRIP?
...
A TAD BUMPY, PERHAPS? WELL, NEVER MIND, HONORED GUESTS.
WHAT IS IT THEY SAY?
IT'S ALL ABOUT THE JOURNEY AND NOT THE DESTINATION!
THE END.

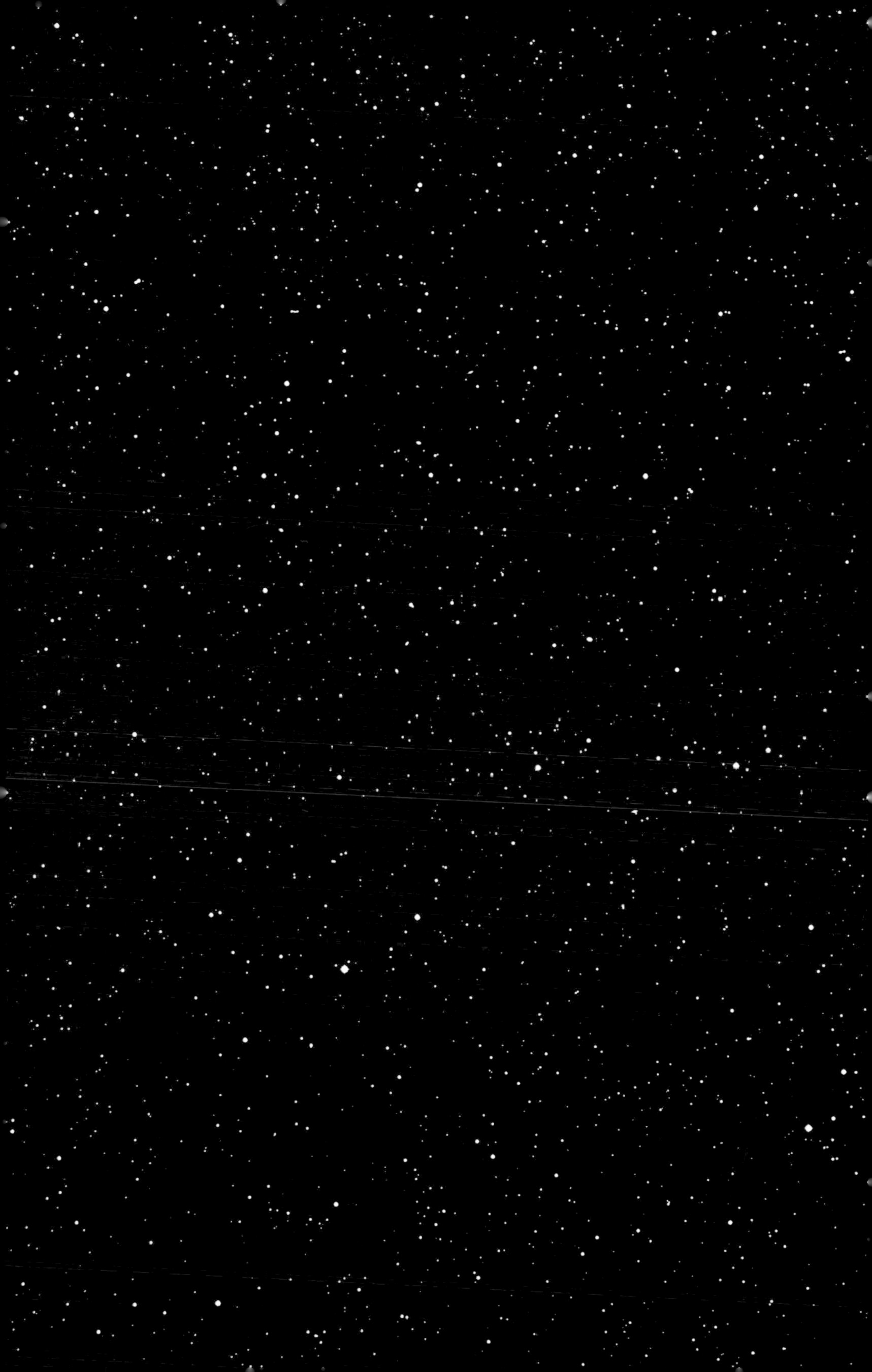

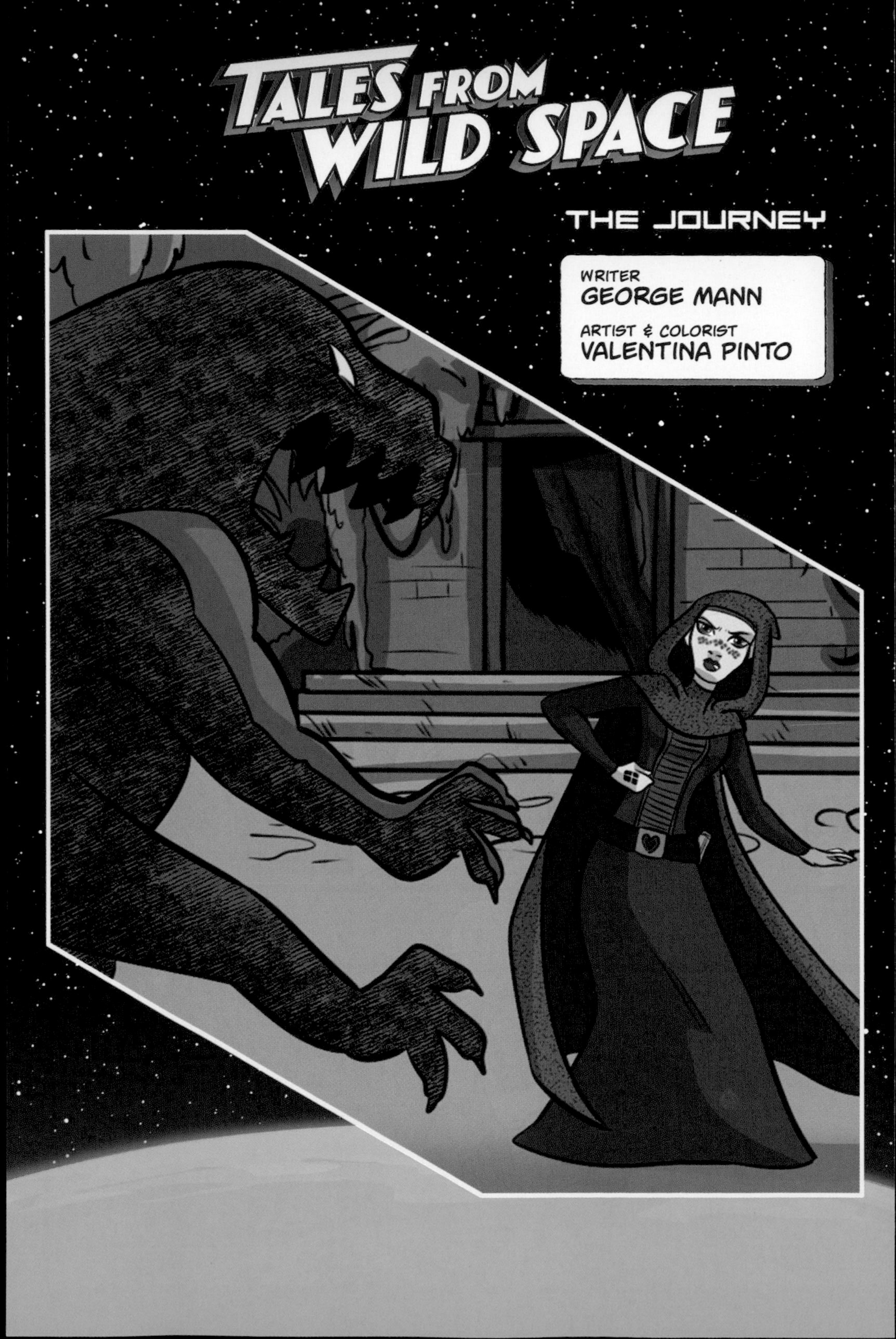
TALES FROM WILD SPACE
THE JOURNEY
WRITER
GEORGE MANN
ARTIST & COLORIST
VALENTINA PINTO

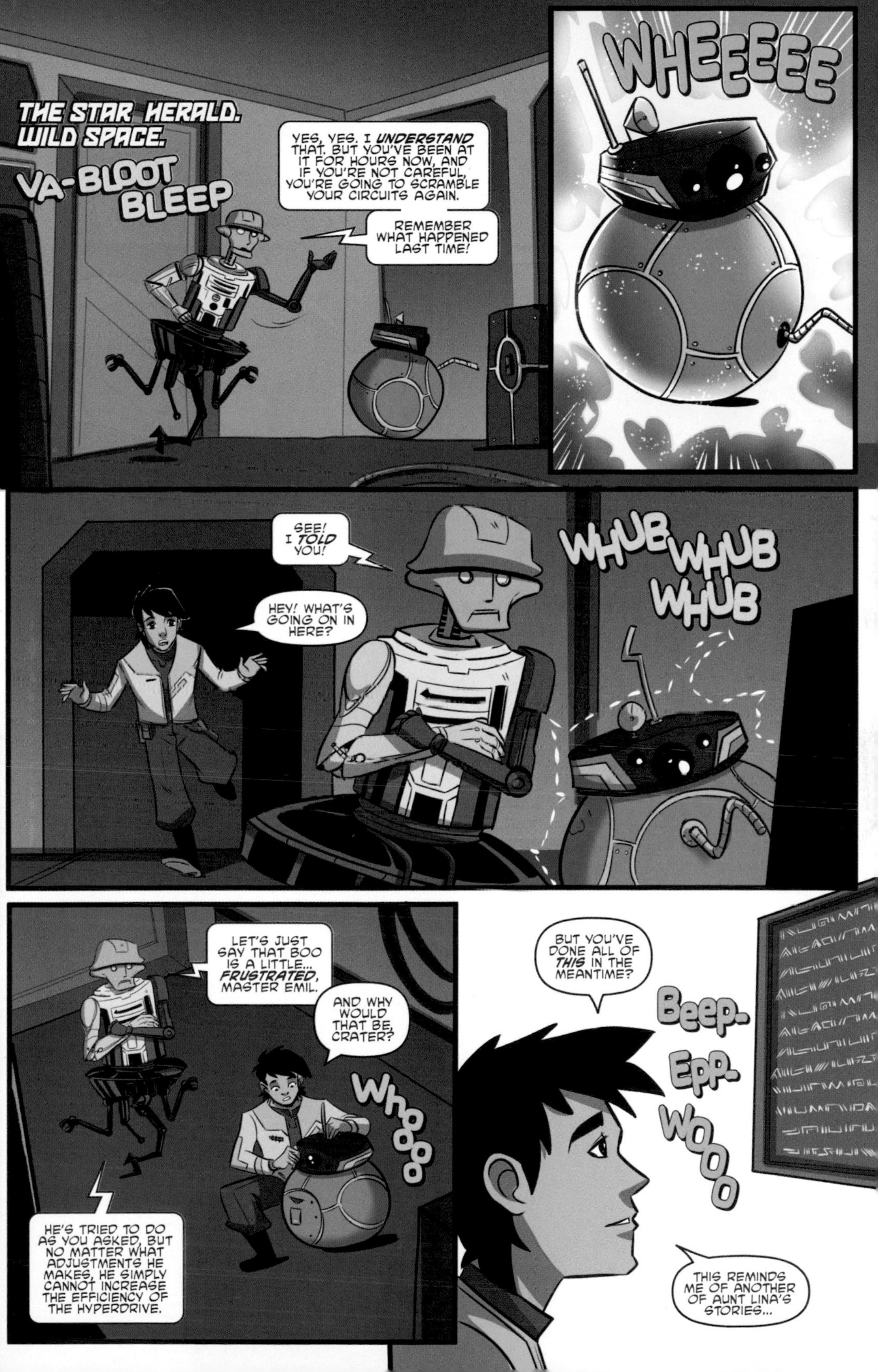

THE STAR HERALD. WILD SPACE.
VA-BLOOT BLEEP
YES, YES. I UNDERSTAND THAT. BUT YOU'VE BEEN AT IT FOR HOURS NOW, AND IF YOU'RE NOT CAREFUL, YOU'RE GOING TO SCRAMBLE YOUR CIRCUITS AGAIN.
REMEMBER WHAT HAPPENED LAST TIME!
WHEEEEEE
SEE! I TOLD YOU!
HEY! WHAT'S GOING ON IN HERE?
WHUB WHUB WHUB
LET'S JUST SAY THAT BOO IS A LITTLE... FRUSTRATED, MASTER EMIL.
AND WHY WOULD THAT BE, CRATER?
Whoooo
HE'S TRIED TO DO AS YOU ASKED, BUT NO MATTER WHAT ADJUSTMENTS HE MAKES, HE SIMPLY CANNOT INCREASE THE EFFICIENCY OF THE HYPERDRIVE.
BUT YOU'VE DONE ALL OF THIS IN THE MEANTIME?
Beep. Epp. Wooo
THIS REMINDS ME OF ANOTHER OF AUNT LINA'S STORIES...

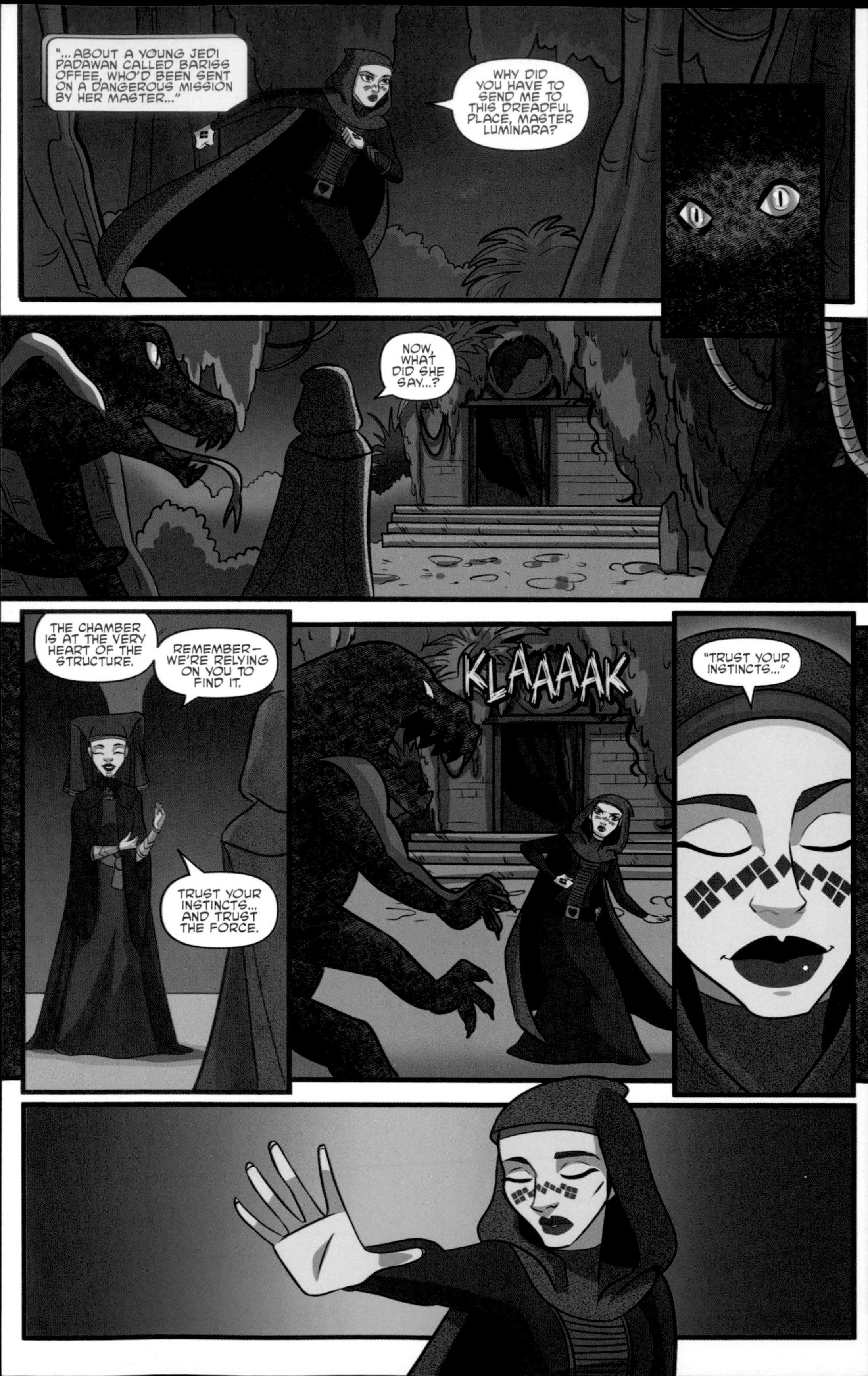
"...ABOUT A YOUNG JEDI PADAWAN CALLED BARISS OFFEE, WHO'D BEEN SENT ON A DANGEROUS MISSION BY HER MASTER..."
WHY DID YOU HAVE TO SEND ME TO THIS DREADFUL PLACE, MASTER LUMINARA?
NOW, WHAT DID SHE SAY...?
THE CHAMBER IS AT THE VERY HEART OF THE STRUCTURE.
REMEMBER— WE'RE RELYING ON YOU TO FIND IT.
TRUST YOUR INSTINCTS... AND TRUST THE FORCE.
KLAAAAK
"TRUST YOUR INSTINCTS..."

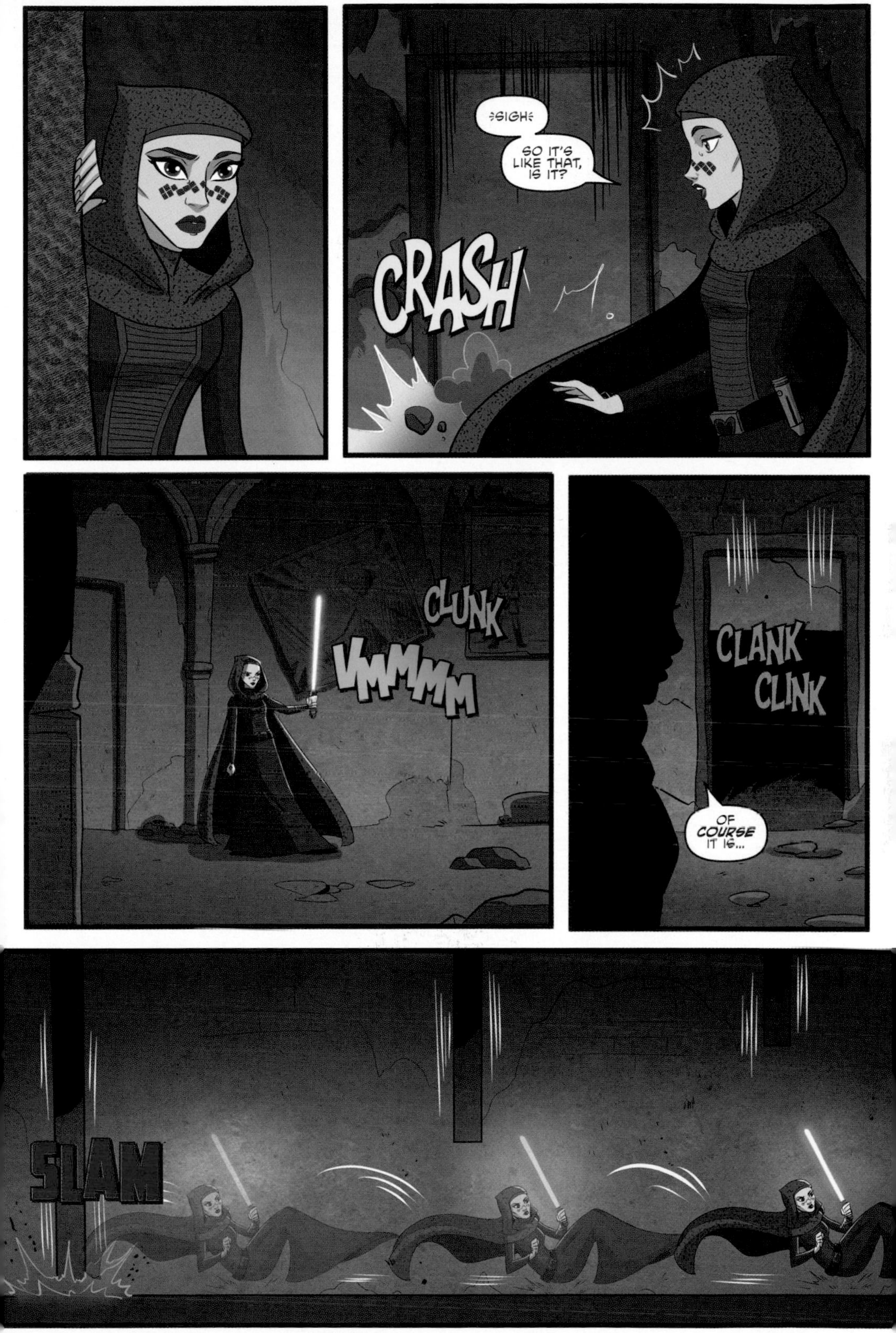

⁼SIGH⁼
SO IT'S LIKE THAT, IS IT?
CRASH
CLUNK
VMMMM
CLANK
CLINK
OF *COURSE* IT IS...
SLAM

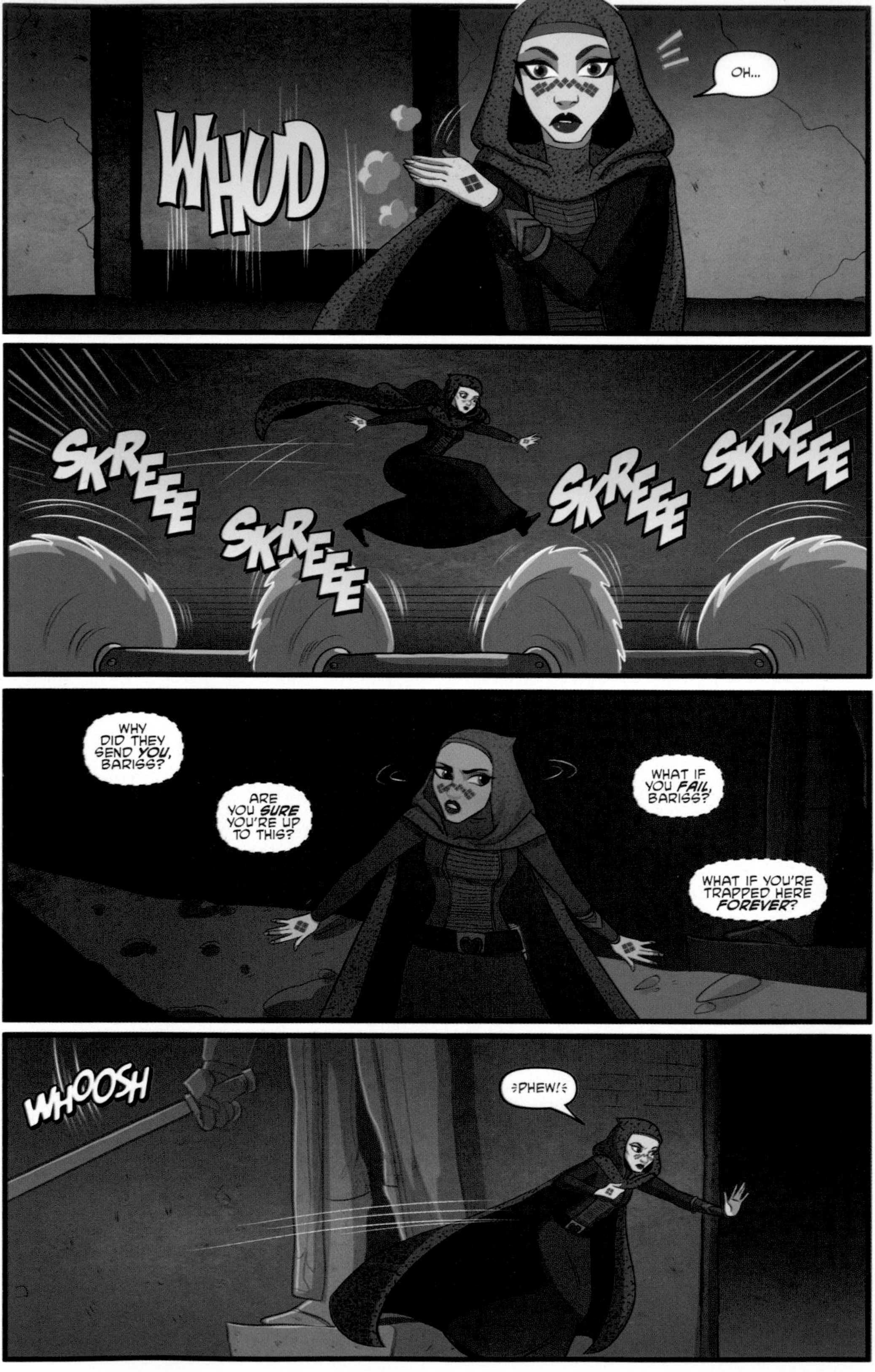
WHUD
OH...
SKREEEE
SKREEEE
SKREEEE
SKREEEE
WHY DID THEY SEND YOU, BARISS?
ARE YOU SURE YOU'RE UP TO THIS?
WHAT IF YOU FAIL, BARISS?
WHAT IF YOU'RE TRAPPED HERE FOREVER?
WHOOSH
PHEW!

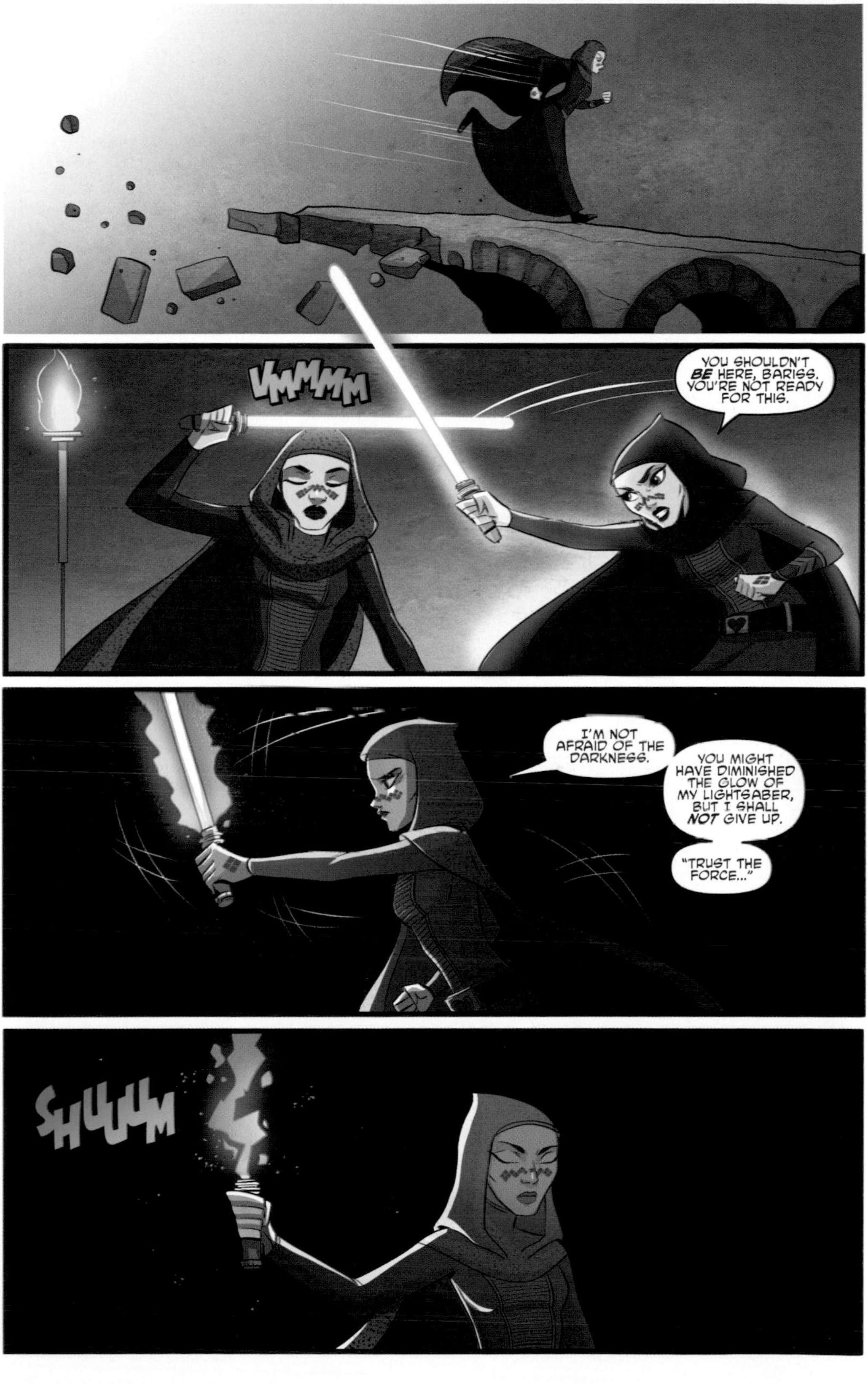
UMMMM
YOU SHOULDN'T BE HERE, BARISS. YOU'RE NOT READY FOR THIS.
I'M NOT AFRAID OF THE DARKNESS.
YOU MIGHT HAVE DIMINISHED THE GLOW OF MY LIGHTSABER, BUT I SHALL NOT GIVE UP.
"TRUST THE FORCE..."
SHUUUM

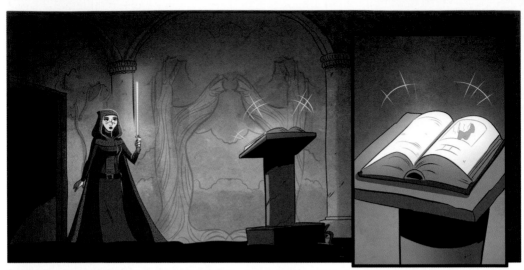

"THE CHAMBER IS AT THE VERY HEART OF THE STRUCTURE.

"REMEMBER— WE'RE RELYING ON YOU TO FIND IT."

I *DID* IT.

NO!

"I'M SORRY, MASTER."

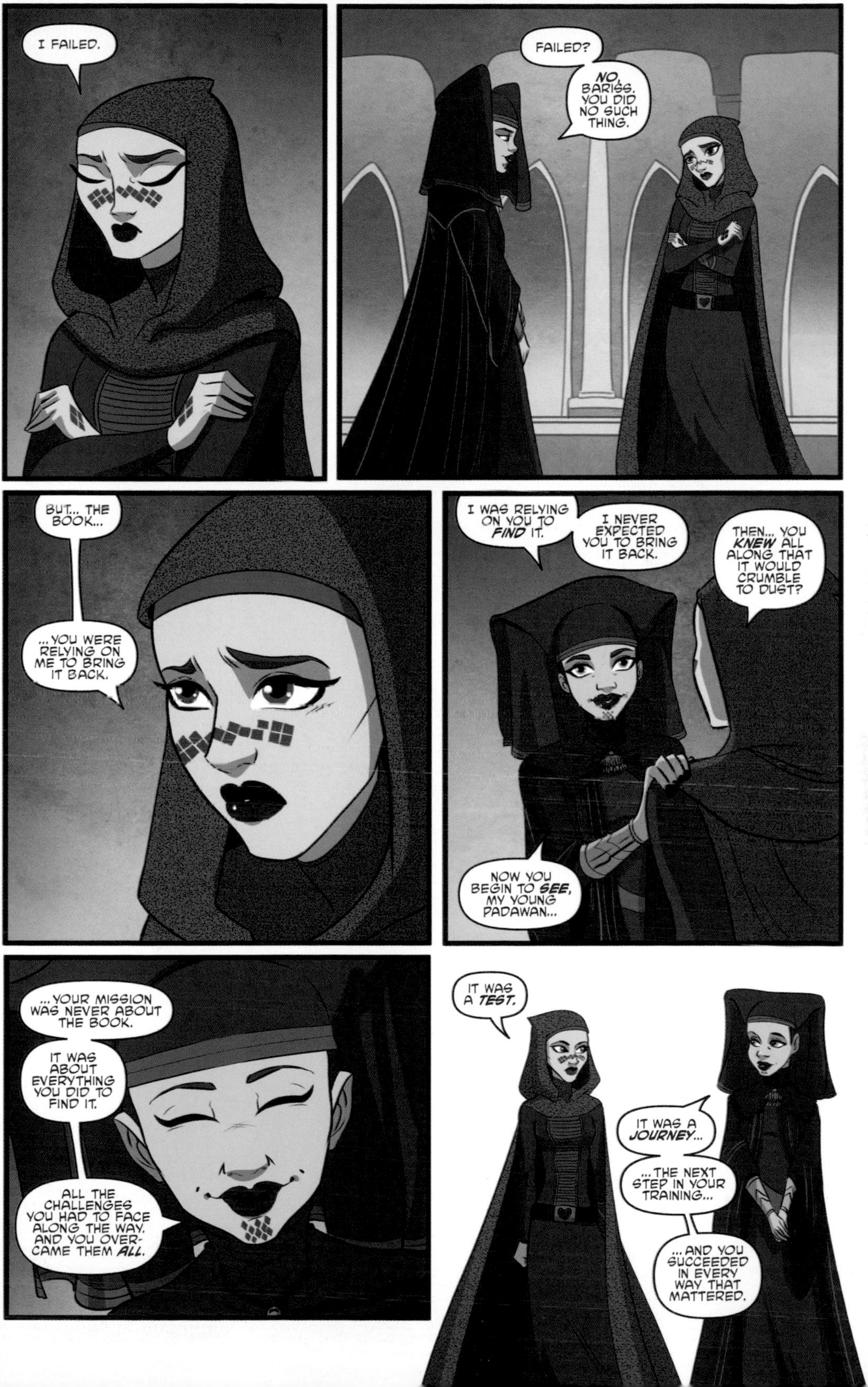
I FAILED.
FAILED?
NO, BARISS. YOU DID NO SUCH THING.
BUT... THE BOOK...
...YOU WERE RELYING ON ME TO BRING IT BACK.
I WAS RELYING ON YOU TO FIND IT.
I NEVER EXPECTED YOU TO BRING IT BACK.
THEN... YOU KNEW ALL ALONG THAT IT WOULD CRUMBLE TO DUST?
NOW YOU BEGIN TO SEE, MY YOUNG PADAWAN...
...YOUR MISSION WAS NEVER ABOUT THE BOOK.
IT WAS ABOUT EVERYTHING YOU DID TO FIND IT.
ALL THE CHALLENGES YOU HAD TO FACE ALONG THE WAY. AND YOU OVERCAME THEM ALL.
IT WAS A TEST.
IT WAS A JOURNEY...
...THE NEXT STEP IN YOUR TRAINING...
...AND YOU SUCCEEDED IN EVERY WAY THAT MATTERED.

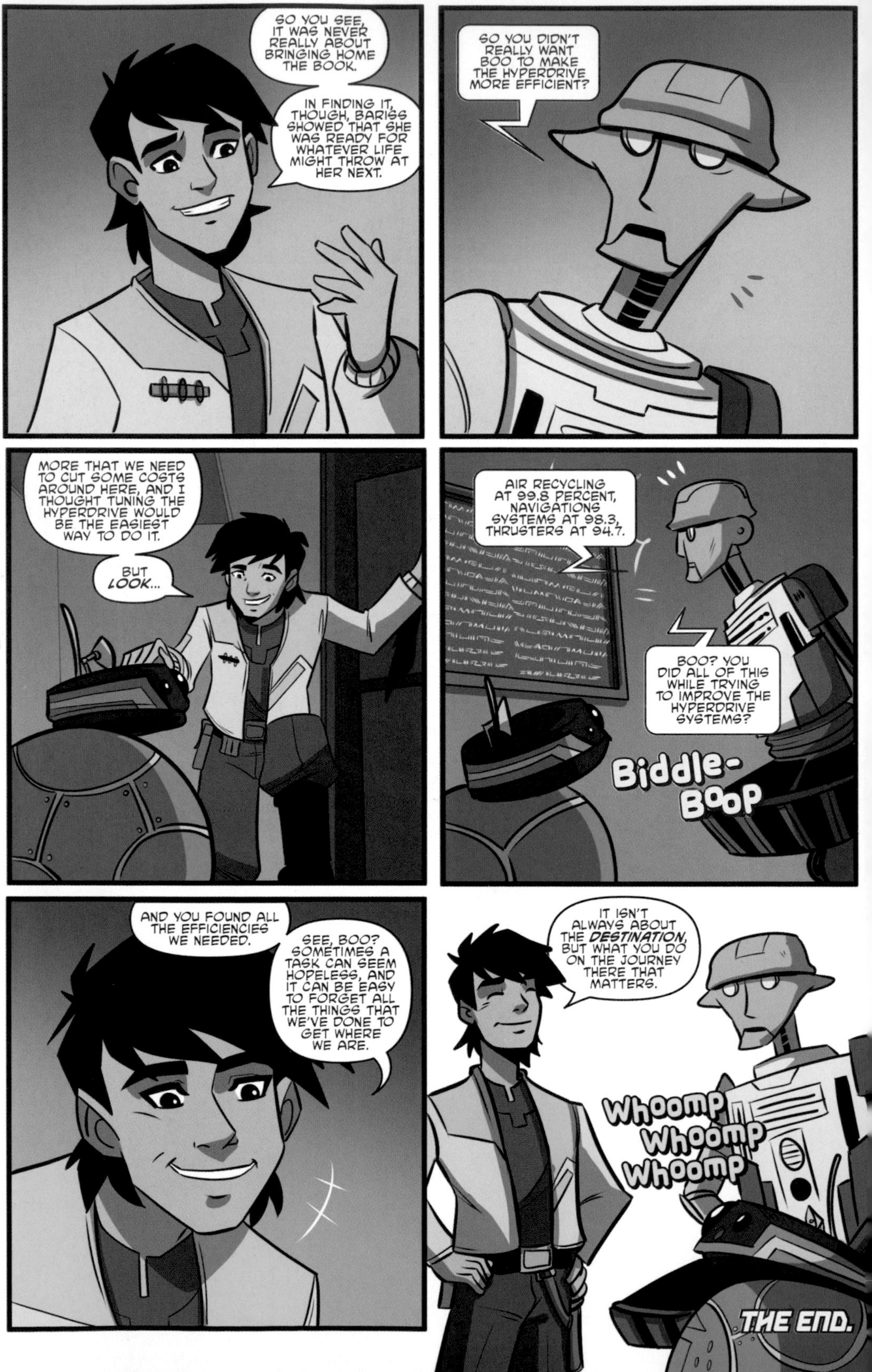
SO YOU SEE, IT WAS NEVER REALLY ABOUT BRINGING HOME THE BOOK.
IN FINDING IT, THOUGH, BARISS SHOWED THAT SHE WAS READY FOR WHATEVER LIFE MIGHT THROW AT HER NEXT.
SO YOU DIDN'T REALLY WANT BOO TO MAKE THE HYPERDRIVE MORE EFFICIENT?
MORE THAT WE NEED TO CUT SOME COSTS AROUND HERE, AND I THOUGHT TUNING THE HYPERDRIVE WOULD BE THE EASIEST WAY TO DO IT.
BUT LOOK...
AIR RECYCLING AT 99.8 PERCENT, NAVIGATIONS SYSTEMS AT 98.3, THRUSTERS AT 94.7.
BOO? YOU DID ALL OF THIS WHILE TRYING TO IMPROVE THE HYPERDRIVE SYSTEMS?
Biddle-Boop
AND YOU FOUND ALL THE EFFICIENCIES WE NEEDED.
SEE, BOO? SOMETIMES A TASK CAN SEEM HOPELESS, AND IT CAN BE EASY TO FORGET ALL THE THINGS THAT WE'VE DONE TO GET WHERE WE ARE.
IT ISN'T ALWAYS ABOUT THE DESTINATION, BUT WHAT YOU DO ON THE JOURNEY THERE THAT MATTERS.
Whoomp Whoomp Whoomp
THE END.

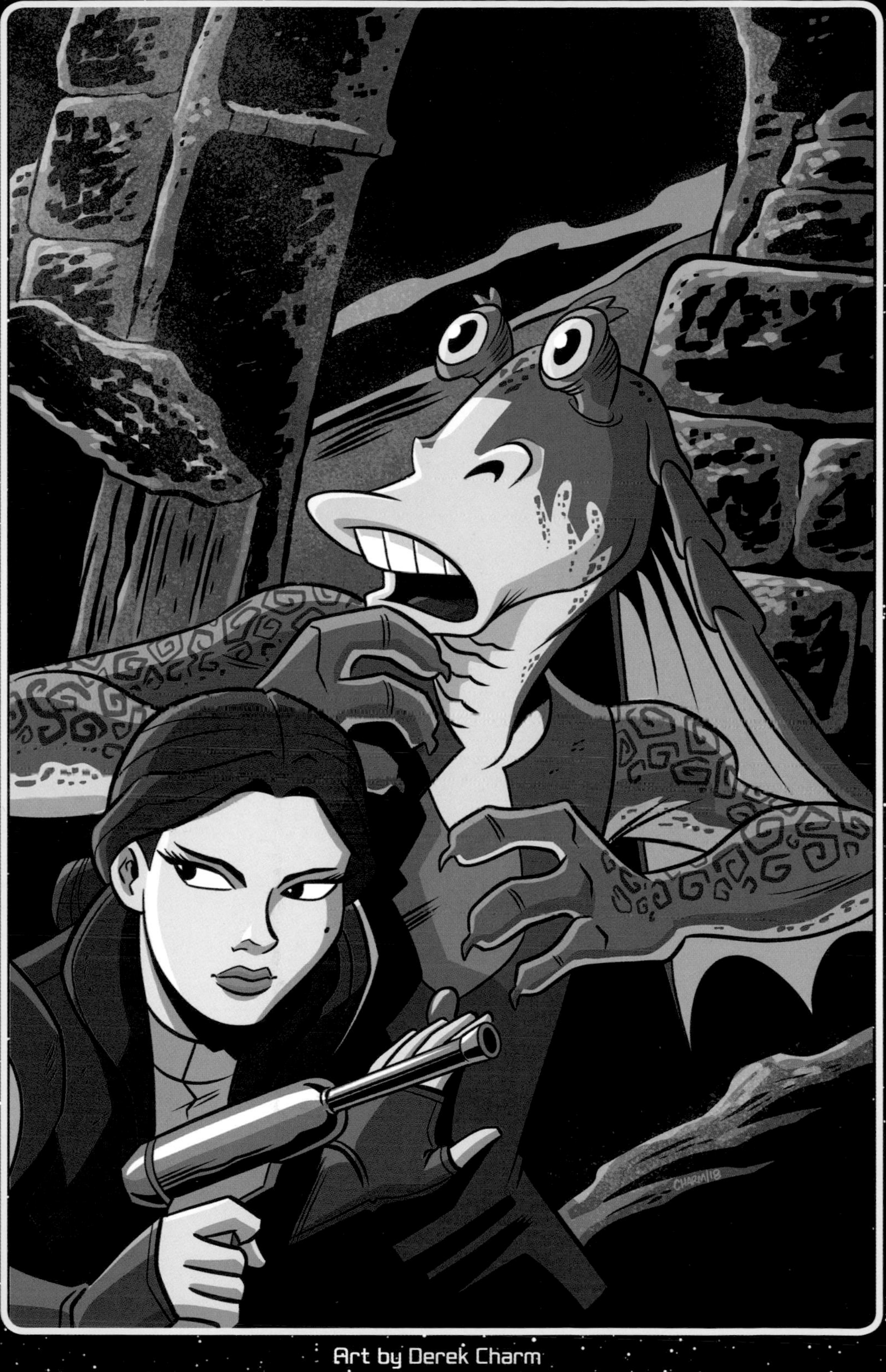

CHARM

Art by Derek Charm

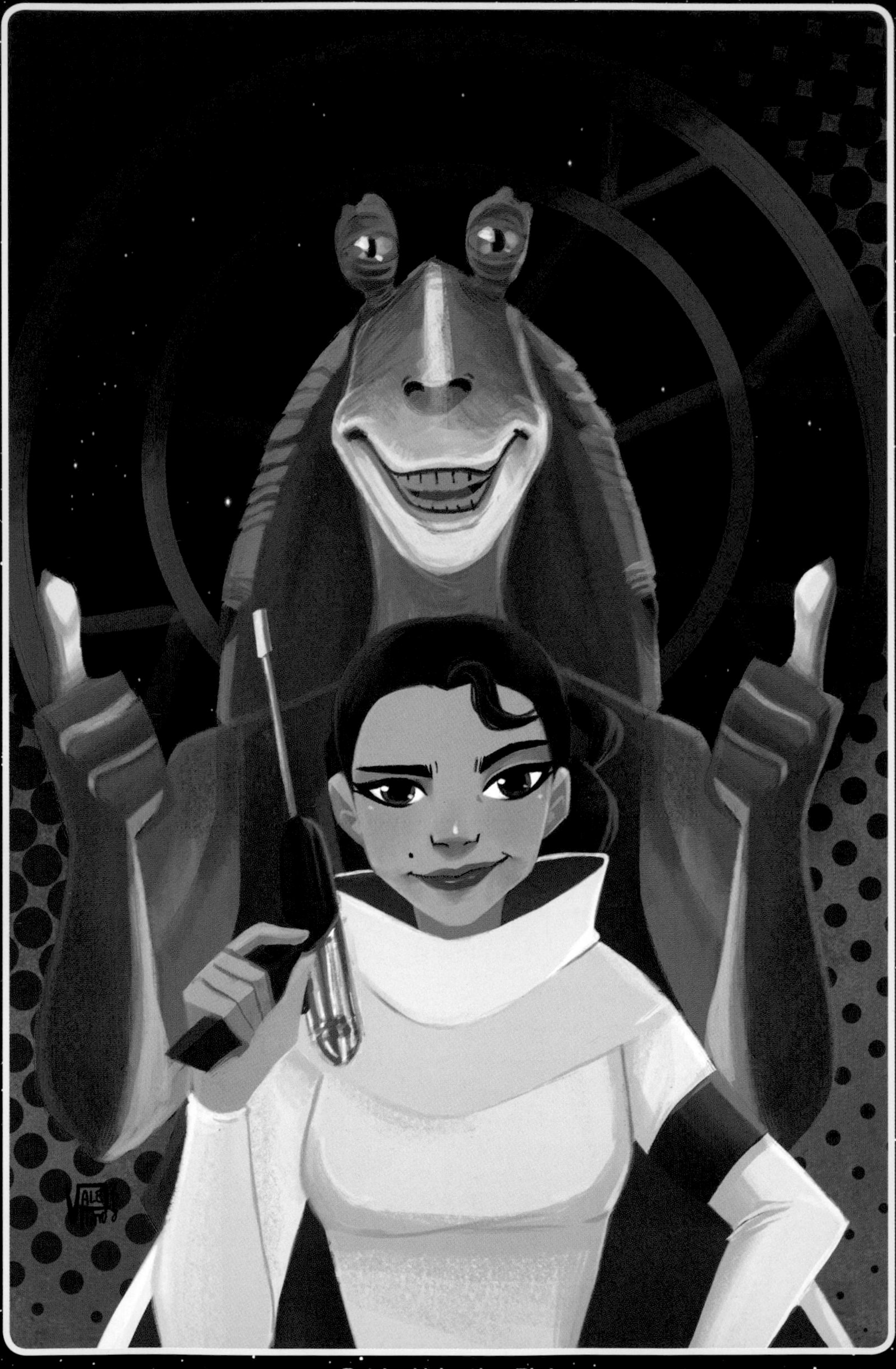

Art by Valentina Pinto

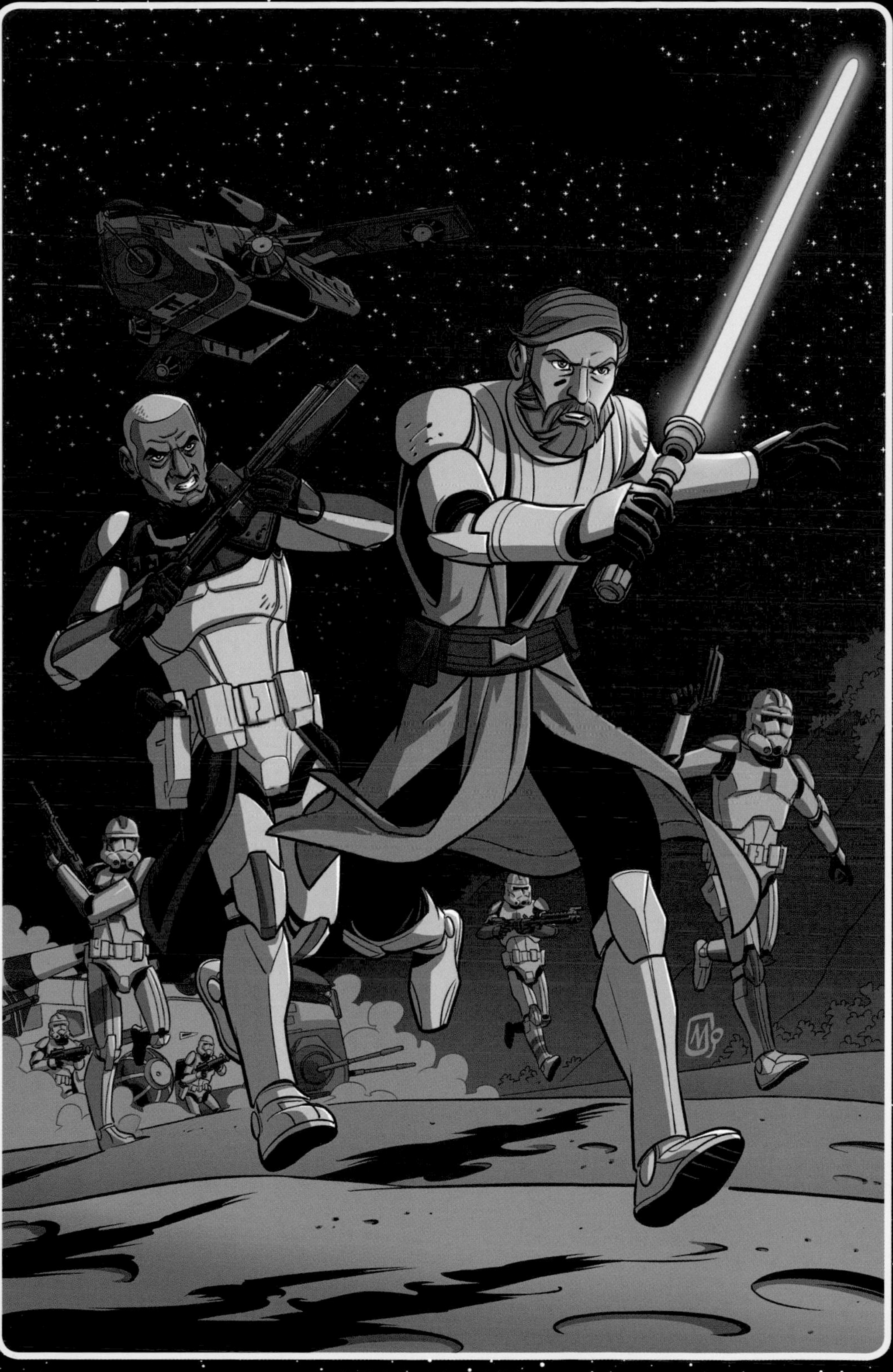

Art by Mauricet

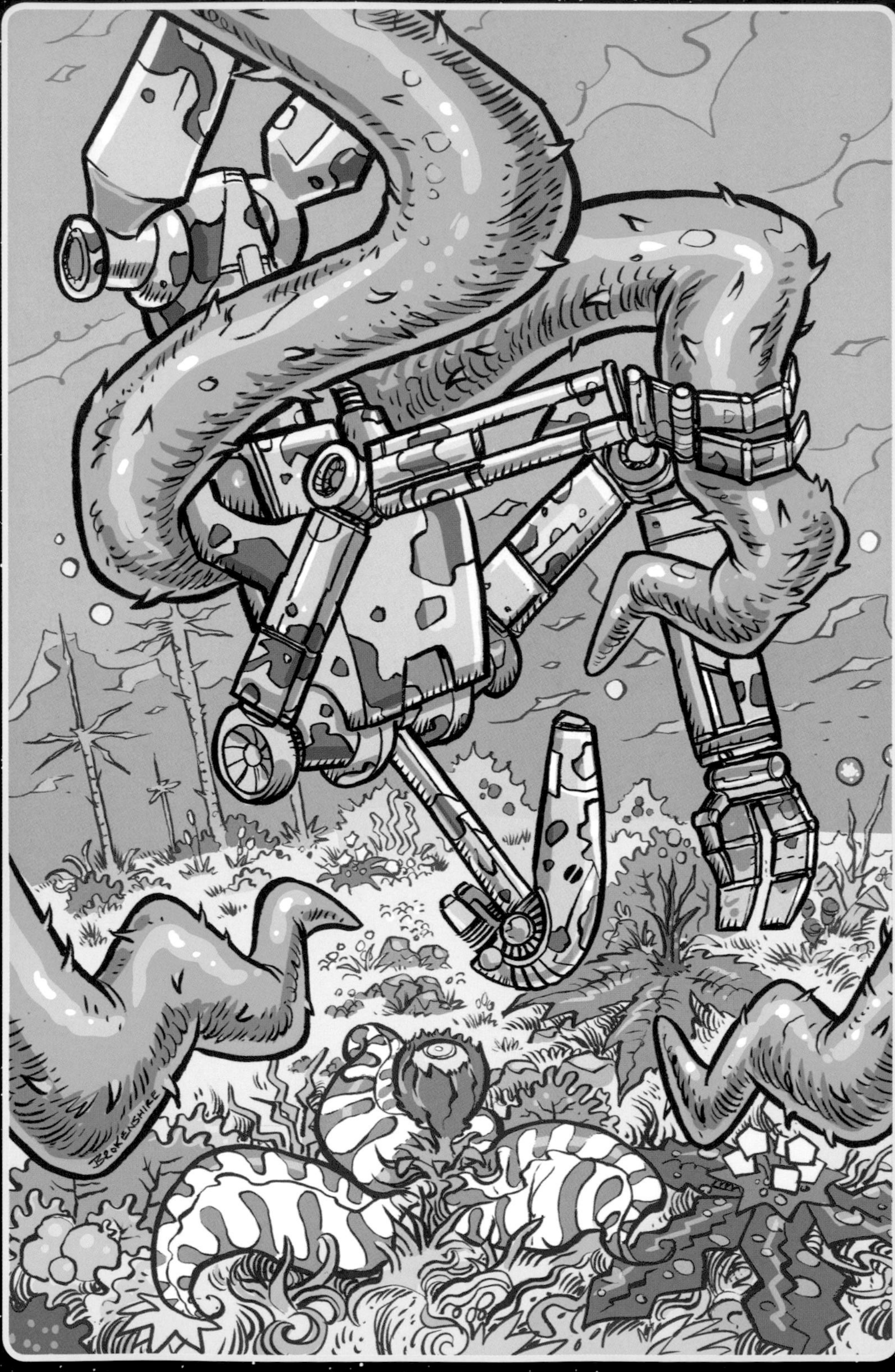
BROKENSHIRE

Art by Nick Brokenshire

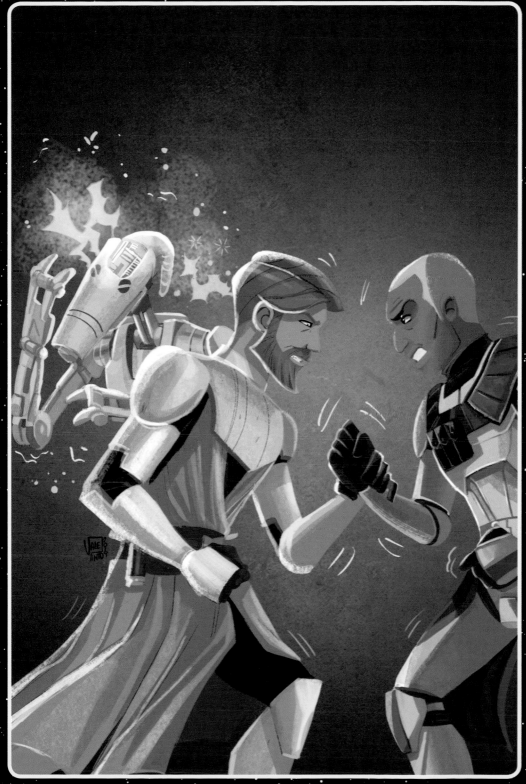

Art by Valentina Pinto

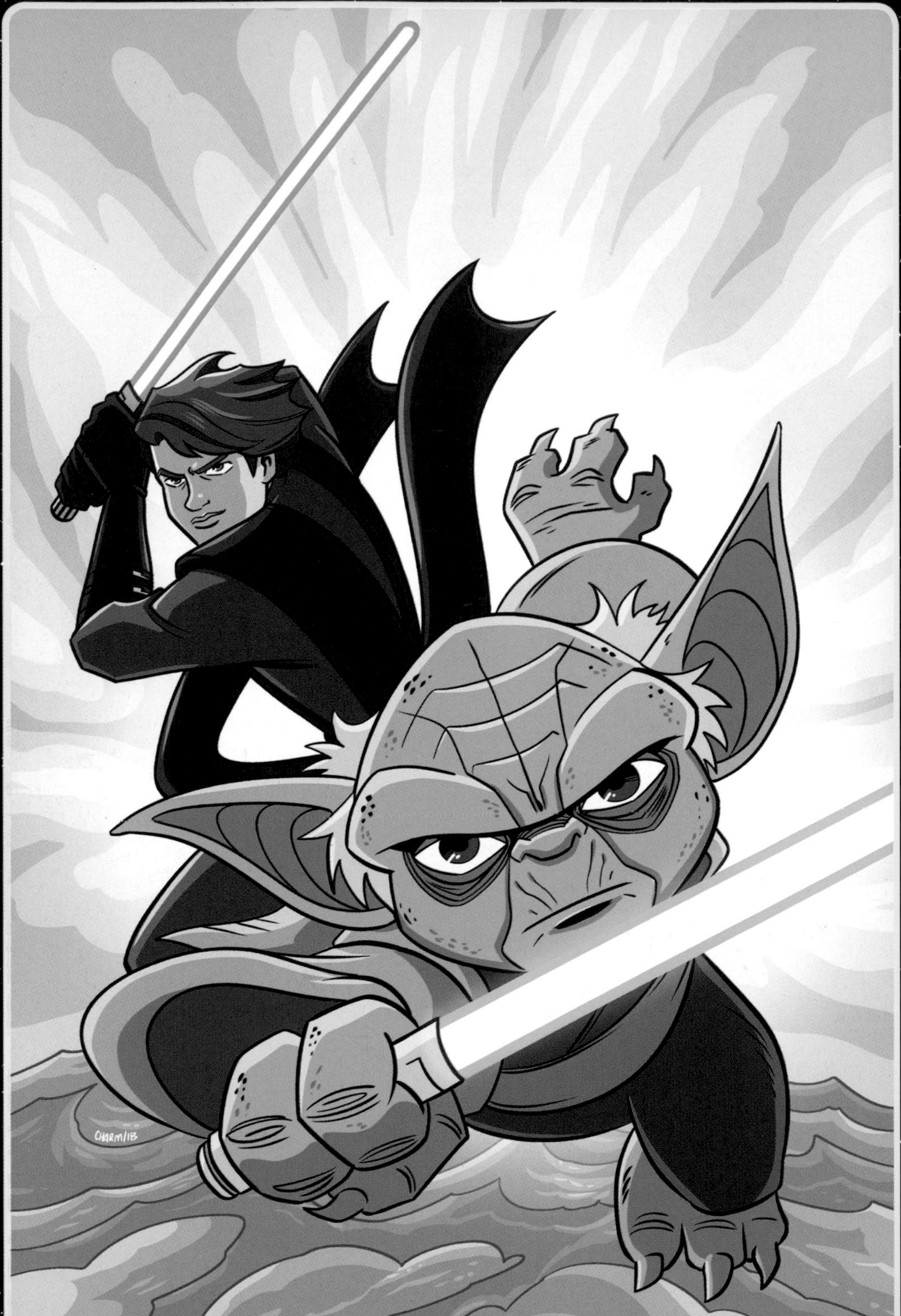
CHARM/18

Art by Derek Charm

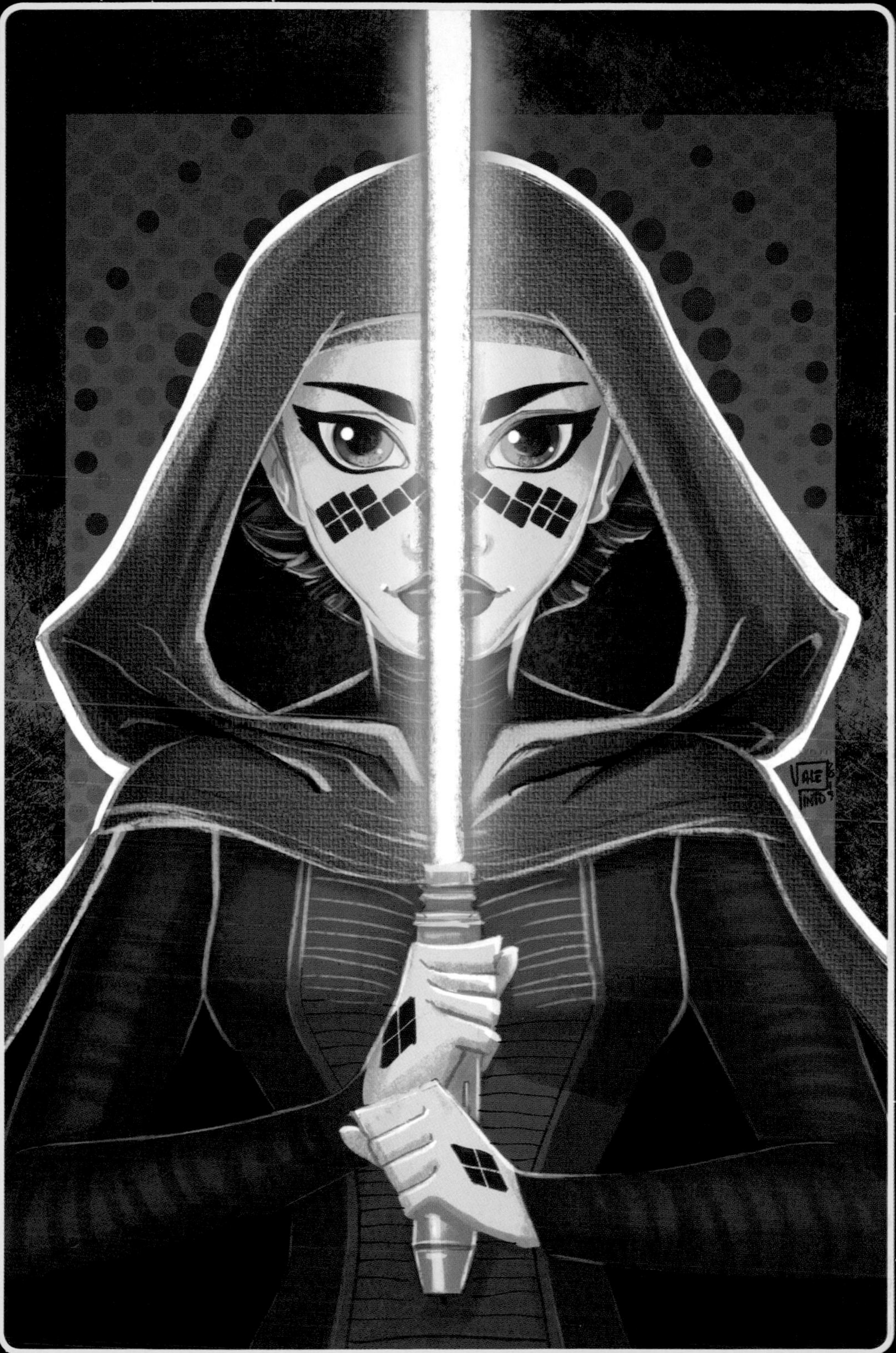
VALE PINTO
Art by Valentina Pinto

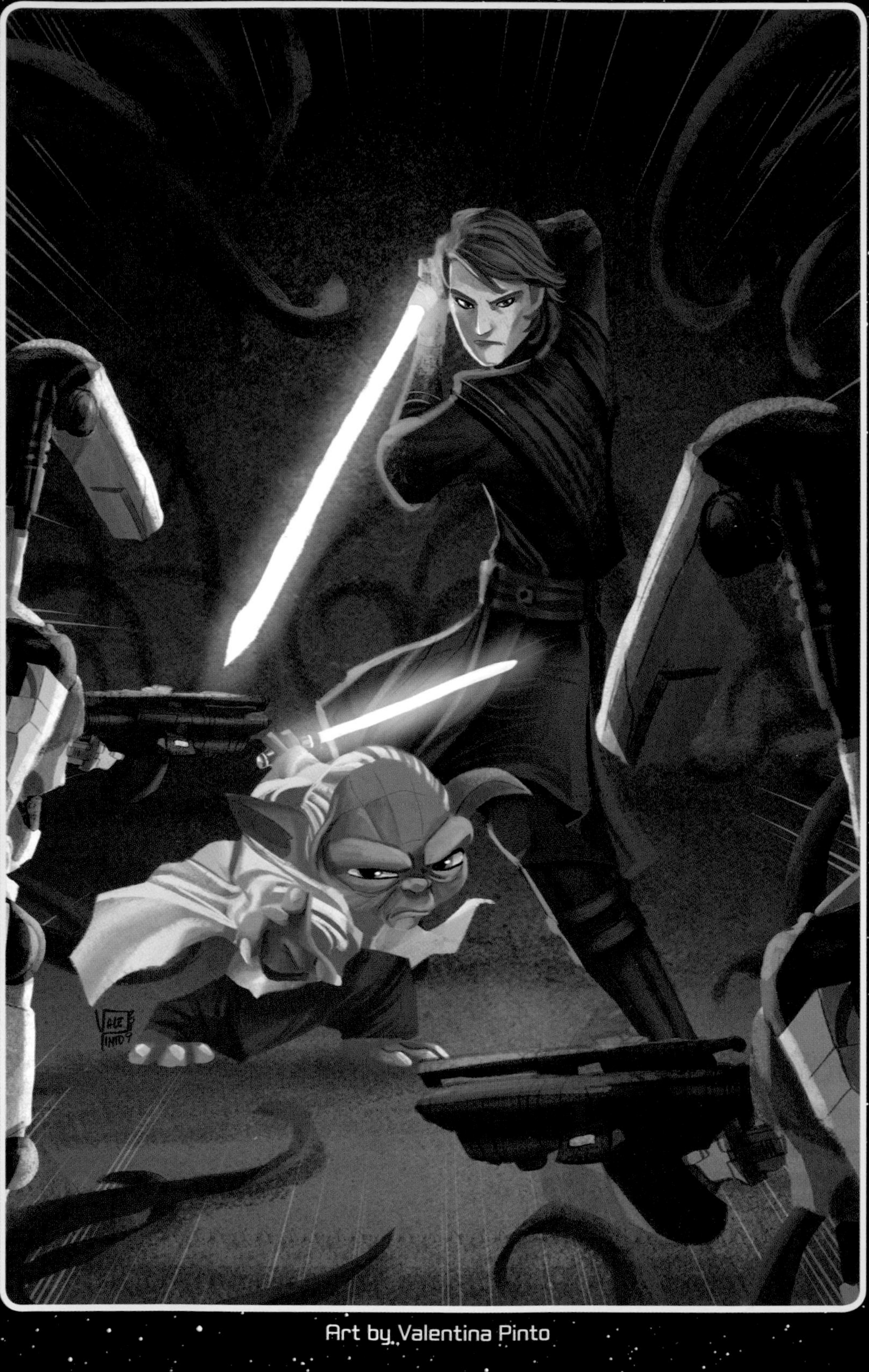

Art by Valentina Pinto